DEMON DAYS
BOOK TWO

DEMON DAYS
BOOK TWO
By Richard Finney
D.L. Snell

Copyright © Richard Finney
Published by Lono Publishing

ISBN 978-1-938457-10-4
FIRST EDITION 2013

Original publication 2011
as DEMON DAYS – Angel of Light

Printed in the United States of America

PRAISE FOR DEMON DAYS

"*Demon Days* by Richard Finney and D.L. Snell is a fresh and rich approach to the age-old battle between good and evil. It's a gripping, visual, pulse-racing read."

—Andrew Neiderman, Author of *The Devil's Advocate*

"*Demon Days* is, by far and away, the best damned horror novel I've read in ages. It's been awhile since anyone has written compelling religious horror, the kind that harks back to *The Exorcist* and *The Omen*. *Demon Days* brings back elements that, for the most part, have been missing from horror novels for a while—compelling characters, and a sense of mystery and suspense. I hope to read anything Finney and Snell write in the future, whether individually or together. Their arrival in the genre is a welcome event!"

—Ray Garton, author of *Live Girls*

"*Demon Days* delivers suspense and pacing that rivals a James Rollins thriller, with stabs of visceral horror worthy of Douglas Clegg and Brian Keene."

—John Kirk, author of *The Talion Moth*

"Inevitably, somebody will try to tell you this book is part *The Da Vinci Code*, part *The Exorcist*, but they will be doing *Demon Days* a grave disservice. Yes, it's a high octane Church-centered conspiracy thriller. Yes, it's a terrifying account of demonic possession. But Finney and Snell have reached beyond those beginnings and have given us a truly important modern horror story. Like the best of T.E.D. Klein, *Demon Days* builds to an awe-inspiring confrontation between our thoroughly modern sensibilities and the supernatural. Finney and Snell will have your full attention right up to the last word."

—Joe McKinney, author of *Apocalypse of the Dead*

READER ACCLAIM FOR DEMON DAYS

4.3 out of 5 Stars! (Amazon.com)

"If you like thrillers and mysteries told at a fast pace but not so fast you're left behind, check it out. The characters (and locations, wow) are well drawn, and the plot is very suspenseful. I really liked the surprises, which were delivered like these writers had an excellent command of the craft. I couldn't put it down. Bravo to the publishers for recognizing a new voice."

"And just when you think you know what's going on in *Demon Days*, the writers throw in a new twist. And these twists come hard and fast."

"The book just sucks you in and doesn't let you come back up for air! The big twist to the book was something that I NEVER saw coming. It was masterfully executed."

"At times, Finney and Snell present the story straightforward, yet other times with descriptive complexity to further crescendo their crisp, chilling writing style. *Demon Days* captures your imagination... It is a wicked good read!"

"I felt like I was on a fast-paced ride wanting to know what was going to happen at the next curve. I now patiently wait for the next edition because I find myself wanting to know where the next curve will be taking me."

—Amazon.com

DEMON DAYS
BOOK TWO

BY

RICHARD FINNEY

D.L. SNELL

LONO PUBLISHING
Encino / California

RICHARD FINNEY

For Brooke, who's had to learn over the years how to live with a Demon.

D.L. SNELL

For my brothers, Andy and Zach, who over the years have done a commendable job curbing their urges to kill me.

The Story Thus Far…

In *DEMON DAYS* we meet Sandy Travis, a news producer for a network TV show. She and her fiancé, Tom Hansen, are involved in a tragic helicopter crash while vacationing in Hawaii.

As a result of the accident, Tom dies… but returns to the living after a Near-Death Experience. Tom believes his N.D.E. changed him for the better.

Sandy is not so sure.

Over the last few years, Father Alan Olsen has been involved in supernatural incidents causing him to believe there is a worldwide conspiracy to usher in the End Days, which if successful, will allow Satan (aka, *the Angel of Light)* to become a physical presence here on earth.

Olsen approaches Sandy for support in proving his cause. Motivated by her fear of something mysterious controlling Tom, Sandy eventually agrees to use her resources to help Father Olsen.

Their investigation uncovers proof of a deadly conspiracy involving Tom as the centerpiece of an assassination plot with apocalyptic implications. But their search for the truth also triggers the killing of innocent people connected to our two protagonists.

At a televised event, meant to signify peace on the planet, shockingly one of our protagonists ends up being demonically possessed and performs a violent act.

Our other protagonist is helpless to change the outcome. This violent act allows the Angel of Light to possess the body of the influential diplomat, John Wolfenson.

Satan is here, walking amongst us.

And only a few people know the truth...

PROLOGUE

As an envoy and a diplomat, John Wolfenson had learned that, in politics, your life should never be your own but the public's. In that way, you could become something greater than yourself.

When he and six other political leaders took to the stage that day at the Western Wall Plaza, the cheers from the crowd physically *moved* him, as if he, too, were shouting—as if they were shouting through him. It moved him to tears.

People had come from all four quarters, and far corners of the earth, whether they followed Jesus, Elohim, or Allah. They all came to witness the day when a conflict as old as time would come to an end. No longer would Arabs and Israelis spill blood over land.

"Instead," John Wolfenson said, booming over loudspeakers to the crowd, "let us celebrate our common ground. Let us usher in a new era of peace and prosperity and, most importantly, let us embrace a time of unity, the well from which eternal hope springs."

After concluding his speech, the envoy introduced the Israeli Prime Minister and the leaders from five Arab countries who had agreed to the peace treaty. Each man, when introduced, soaked up the wild adulation of the crowd. Then all six of them settled into their chairs and began the final act of the peace agreement. Signature documents of the treaty were distributed amongst the participants, and the men picked up their pens.

John glanced toward a roped-off area next to the stage where VIPs watched the proceedings. The envoy wanted to get a reaction from his wife, Patricia—wanted her to know this wasn't just for him. But John didn't see her. He saw the news producer, Sandy Travis, instead. She was staring right at him.

He had run into her on his way to the stage and had tried his best not to be unsettled. John had known Sandy for a long time and had invited her to cover the event, and to conduct an exclusive interview with him afterward. But just an hour before the ceremony, his security officials had warned him that Sandy's fiancé, Tom Hansen, might make an attempt on John's life that very day. It was Sandy herself who had reported Tom's suspicious behavior to the Israel Security Agency, the Shin Bet.

The envoy approached the table to say a few friendly words to the leaders as they traded signature copies and continued to sign. But before he said a word, John noticed a flurry of activity amongst the spectators. Someone had attempted to assassinate him before, in Tel Aviv, so he had become sensitive to signs of unrest. To the dignitaries around him, he tried not to reveal what his eyes had picked up on—Shin Bet agents on the move, weaving their way throughout the crowd, all converging on a man moving intently toward the stage.

John felt the briefest stab of fear as the man reached into his jacket for something, but then security agents swarmed the man, and they disappeared with him into the throng of spectators.

The envoy tried to shrug it off. He had been working tirelessly on this treaty for years, and today it would finally be signed. It was the greatest day of his life. He would not let anyone get in the way of it.

The Israeli Prime Minister signed the final document, and then, prompted by Envoy Wolfenson, he and the Arab leaders gathered at the center of the stage for one more photo op. Each leader embraced the other, and they raised their hands in triumph.

The ocean of people beyond the platform cheered, and it was over. The leaders started to leave the stage. John followed behind them, waving to the audience, who waved back with flags, some bearing the Star of David, others flying the banners of Arab countries in various striations of red, green, black, and white.

He turned to the steps leading down from the stage, when suddenly the Prime Minister and Arab leaders ahead of him were pushed aside, and Sandy Travis came barreling between them up the stairs.

Her eyes had turned pitch black.

John glimpsed the wake she had left behind her, the VIPs still reeling and stepping back, revealing Sandy's cameraman, who lay bleeding on the stone tile of the plaza next to his broken camera.

A shot rang out from one of the surrounding buildings, and Sandy stumbled backward as her shirt billowed out. The bullet didn't stop her though. She caught her balance and rushed forward again, raising her arm, and John saw something sharp gleaming in her hand. He tried to react, but was too late—she was stabbing him in the neck, even as two bullet holes opened in her throat, and another one in her chest.

Both John and Sandy fell, one left, the other right. John woke up a second later, lying on the stage.

He heard shouting and hundreds of screams, saw people in the plaza, just scrambling, blurry shapes. And he saw Sandy Travis lying across from him.

A trail of blood ran between them, connected them. It was inseparable what blood was whose. Except for the blood on the shard of camera lens.

That blood was John's.

Spatters of it led back to his neck.

He reached up to hold the wound in his throat, and something hot and thick gushed against his hand.

A page fluttered down from the table on the stage. It had been signed. All six leaders, all six signatures.

The page landed and stuck in the blood.

Sandy stared across at John, and the blackness began to fade from her eyes.

Security agents swarmed in around them, guns drawn, leather shoes and boots stomping, clomping, shuffling this way and that.

"Mr. Envoy—Mr. Envoy!"

John's eyes remained locked on Sandy's through the ever-shifting assembly of legs and shoes.

Briefly, the horde parted as a man shoved his way through, shouting, "I'm a priest!" The man, who wore a cassock and appeared to be blind, knelt beside Sandy. They said something to each other that John couldn't hear, and then the priest began to perform the last rites.

"May the Lord in His love and mercy help you with the grace of the Holy Spirit..."

Two paramedics came to John's side and rolled him over so that he was staring up through a tunnel of people to the bright, bright sun, and he could barely blink.

"May the Lord who frees you from sin save you and raise you up..."

And John began to rise into the light. Everything sounded farther and farther away, and all he felt was warmth.

Then a shadow stepped in front of the light.

———

PATRICIA WOLFENSON, THE ENVOY'S WIFE, paced the hallway outside her husband's private room at Balshem Medical Center in Jerusalem. She had been joined by friends, her husband's staff, and some of their family. Though none would admit it, they all expected bad news. The gathering fell silent when Dr. Diamant stepped out to tell Patricia that her husband was going to survive the attack.

"You're telling me John is going to be okay?"

"Yes. But I don't have to tell you that your husband is lucky to be alive. In fact, for a minute there, he was clinically dead."

"Can I see him?"

The doctor allowed her into his room, but only for a few minutes.

"Honey," she said, rushing to her husband's bedside. "Thank God! I don't know what I would have done without you."

Wolfenson grinned. "Oh, Pat. You'd be thrilled to finally get a better Bridge partner."

She forced a smile for his sake, but tears began to run down her cheeks. Wolfenson raised her hand to his lips and kissed it. "Honey, I want you to get ahold of whoever's in charge of the kitchen and demand that I get a slice of apple pie immediately. Tell them it's for the man who just brought peace to the Mideast."

Patricia wiped away the tears, kissed her husband's forehead and left to get his dessert.

Wolfenson motioned for one of his bodyguards to let a group of five men and one woman into his private room. The group had arrived seconds ago, as if somehow they knew the envoy had awakened.

In the hallway, Patricia watched the group file into the room. She turned to her husband's long-time press liaison, Rick Walsh.

"Who are those people?"

"I don't know," he said. "I've never seen them before in my life."

The last man to enter the room, Dr. Fincher, shut the door, and what happened in the hall no longer mattered.

From his bed, Wolfenson extended his right hand. Dr. Fincher was the first to kiss it.

"It is so good to finally have you amongst us, my Angel of Light."

As the next person in the congregation knelt in worship, Wolfenson looked out the window. The sky had darkened and had begun to rain. Lightning struck in the distance.

The envoy smiled and turned back to Dr. Fincher.

"What a beautiful day to be alive."

CHAPTER 1

A LL GREAT PLANS TAKE TIME. Those words had become a mantra for Etan Vlessel. He repeated them now as he stood at his bathroom mirror, inserting a color contact lens.

All great plans take time.

Since birth, complete heterochromia had colored his left eye brown, his right one green. His mother, whom he barely remembered, once said the green was a transplant. Oftentimes she forced him to close his eyelid, and to keep it closed. Because, she said, she didn't trust the stranger inside him.

Over the years, Etan had learned to use a color lens to make one eye match. *Which* eye depended on the occasion. Green, for example, helped seduce a target—perhaps for its feline aloofness and pride—whereas brown better suited business deals.

Tonight, he had scheduled a meeting at the Allier Café; so tonight the eyes of his mirror-self would be brown.

On at least three occasions, Etan had studied the Allier Café from across the street, but had never stepped foot inside. A full house of customers kept the staff so busy that, by closing time, he would be just another dirty cup to clean.

Hopefully the same would be true of the man he was meeting; not a single crumb for the police.

"Patience is a virtue," his father had often said. Of course the old man had no patience, especially for Etan.

What his father would have thought of his occupation, he never could decide. At the very least, the old man would have admired his business acumen and unholy patience.

Nearly two years ago, Etan, a foreigner, had leased a house in a little French town practically in the shadow of the basilica in Nice. Two years on the dot, because he needed ample time to learn the culture, time to infiltrate the black market as an artifacts dealer.

Now, with that term elapsed, he could almost smell the vellum of the relic he sought.

He arrived one hour before the meeting to secure his parking space in a sanitation lane near the café. The alley served a row of stores, all of which had closed for the evening. Etan had staked out the area previously and had discovered that poor lighting and the stink of trash discouraged thru traffic.

He parked in the alley and snuffed the only light.

Fifteen minutes till the meeting, he entered the café. The hostess seated him on the patio near the wrought-iron railing, and he did not protest, nor request anything special.

On the sidewalk, beyond the foliate and floral ironwork and rails, troubadours—local street musicians—stopped at the Allier to sing a pop song for tips.

Etan ordered a cappuccino and resisted the itch in his eye. He couldn't displace the contact, for even partial heterochromia creeped people out.

The man with whom Etan was meeting, Carlo Venova, worked as a travel agent, although not in the business of getaways. He specialized in moving ancient contraband from one country to another.

The black market in ancient artifacts grossed billions of dollars per year, but as with any illegal trade the problem was shipping and handling. Recently, many countries had beefed up their customs department, hiring more inspectors at airports and other checkpoints across the map.

According to his reputation, Carlo Venova had worked as a travel agent in the black market for nearly two decades.

Being the shrewd businessman that he was, Carlo had checked Etan's connections before agreeing to meet at the café. Obviously those connections had checked out: Carlo had finally arrived, and only a few minutes late.

Etan waved him over.

Earlier, when they first spoke on the phone, Etan had introduced himself as Paul Seeger, which had been his alias since relocating to France. So when Carlo shook his hand and asked if he were Paul, Etan said yes, he was, and they were no longer strangers.

Carlo sat and took up more than his fair share of the table. "How did you know it was me?" he asked with an Italian accent, thick as the leather of his shoes.

Etan said, "Oliver Neumann described you. You know Oliver, yes?"

"How did he describe me?"

Etan smiled and appraised Carlo's ruffled suit jacket and comb-over, and the deep, dark eye sockets with mere shallows of sleep. They looked like the eyes of a fish not long for the ice.

"He said you would be the one who looked like an unmade bed."

Carlo stifled a laugh, and then said, "Screw him. Like he's some fashion plate to be talking about me."

He ordered an espresso and watched the troubadours pack up and move to the next café.

"I checked on you," Carlo said. "You've moved some pretty heavy-duty trinkets. You should have come to me before; I could have given you a better rate."

"I didn't know you then," Etan said, then took a sip from his cappuccino.

"What kind of stuff do you have?"

"A gilded wood pharaoh. Looted from a dig in Cairo."

"How big? How heavy?"

"Not heavy at all. It would be the same size as a Barbie doll... if Barbie weren't anorexic."

"Piece of cake."

"Yeah? Good. So far no problems with this item. We slipped it out of the country from the same man-made tunnels Palestinians use to smuggle weapons into Gaza. Getting it into Israel was the only hairy leg."

"You have it now?" Carlo asked.

Etan raised his cup in a toast. He also winked involuntarily. Cursed lens.

The travel agent didn't seem to notice. "Okay, so where do you want to move it?"

Etan said, "We have a buyer over in New York."

The waiter served Carlo an espresso, which he downed in a single gulp. Etan observed that he gripped the tiny cup with his thumb and middle finger; half of his forefinger was gone, but none of its hair.

"I have a source who will get it to Washington, D.C., no problem," Carlo said after the waiter had wandered off. "You get it to New York from there. What else do you have?"

"Why don't we start with this and see how it goes."

"Okay."

"What's your price?"

Etan pretended to be appalled by Carlo's initial quote, and he spent twenty minutes negotiating, making Carlo really work to justify his cost. Etan knew the more he dickered over money, the more legitimate he would seem.

"Okay, so take me to the goods," Carlo said after they had closed the deal.

Etan paid for the drinks with cash, and led the travel agent toward the sanitation lane. At first, Carlo expressed surprise that Etan had trusted the item to a parked van, but Etan assured him that a business associate was guarding the artifact.

At the dark opening of the alleyway, Etan stopped. So did Carlo.

"Ah, hell," Etan said, "the streetlight must have burned out."

"Where's your car?"

"It's the van. You see it?"

"Yeah, yeah, I see it now."

Etan whistled but no passenger emerged from the vehicle. "He better not be asleep or he's fired. If he's out getting coffee and he left the statue unattended, he's a dead man." He turned to Carlo. "You want to wait here while I get your money and the item?"

"No, too exposed. I'll come with you, no problem."

At the van, Etan moved to the driver's side and saw what he already knew: no one sat inside. "He's a dead man," he announced.

"Do you think he ripped you off?"

"I guess we shall find out."

He pressed the unlock button on his key fob, then threw open the back doors. The van's interior light illuminated the carpeted cargo hold, which accommodated a leather suitcase and a small object wrapped and taped up in a green towel. Both men breathed a sigh of relief.

"So my business associate is an idiot but not a thief," Etan said. He opened the suitcase. Amongst some papers and leather-bound books sat several stacks of bundled cash.

Carlo smiled and pretended to smell the money from where he stood.

Etan pointed to the towel. "While I count out your share, why don't you check out the statue, tell me if you've seen anything more beautiful?"

As Carlo peeled the masking tape from the cloth, Etan reached into the suitcase and withdrew a syringe.

"This isn't a pharaoh," Carlo said as he unwrapped the small idol. "It's a f—"

Etan injected him in the neck.

Instantly, the Italian collapsed into his arms. Etan lifted him into the back of the van and rested the body atop the object in the towel, which really was a Barbie doll.

He latched the suitcase and prepared to shut the back doors when he heard footsteps and voices echoing behind him.

A group of figures walked into the alley, talking and laughing and carrying musical instruments.

The troubadours from the café.

They were using the lane to get to their next gig.

Etan shut the back doors. Without a glance behind him, he climbed into the driver's seat, fired up the engine, and turned his head to back up—and to hide his face as the musicians passed him by.

————

CARLO VENOVA OPENED HIS EYES. For a split second he thought he was still in the dark alley—but then someone struck a match on the other side of the basement; Carlo sat duct-taped to a chair.

The man, whoever he was, stood at a tiered table, lighting candles: votives, pillars, white and black, over two dozen in all, and each cluster elevated differently on the tiers.

One by one, the flames illuminated the man. Carlo recognized him, though "Paul Seeger" had changed out of his business clothes into a simple black T-shirt and jeans.

"What are you doing?" Carlo asked.

Etan lit the last few candles, then shook out the match. Sulfur lingered in the air, but one of the candles quickly overpowered it with the essences of frankincense and myrrh. Etan breathed in the scents.

"Is this about money?" Carlo asked. "Fine. I will give you money. Let's talk about this. How much do you want?"

"It is not about money," Etan said. "It's about history."

"History?!" Carlo noticed something dangling from a silver chain around his captor's neck, but he couldn't quite make out what it was.

"Yes," Etan said, "history. Medieval specifically. Recent history as well. And if you don't answer me truthfully, my thieving Italian friend, *you're* history."

One corner of the basement, far from the candles, harbored pure darkness. Etan disappeared into it, and Carlo heard him rummaging for something.

"I don't know why you're doing this," the travel agent said, raising his voice and hoping it wouldn't crack. "I thought we had a deal. Don't you think I can be of better service working for you rather than... this?"

Etan reappeared with a wooden side table, handcrafted and at least two hundred years old. He placed the table in front of Carlo. Then, on top of it, he set two human skulls.

Carlo's gut tightened. He had transported enough bones that he could authenticate the ones staring at him now.

Each had something engraved into its forehead. Carlo knew Latin, but couldn't concentrate; he had other things on his mind. Yet for some reason, he managed to register the grammatical declension of the phrase, which made it a sentence fragment.

Etan petted one of the skulls as if it were a cat. "Carlo, I want you to say hello to your black market friend Oliver Neumann."

He moved his hand to the other skull. "And this gentleman... I believe you know him as Samir Droeger, the trader who hired you to move a very special item. Do you recognize these two men?"

Although any familiar feature had been boiled off of the bone, Carlo certainly knew Neumann and Droeger. He wanted to believe the skulls were props, part of Etan's act, but he couldn't. So he nodded. Yes, he had known these men.

"That's the answer I expected," Etan said. "Ours is practically a family business, is it not?" He bent so that his face hovered just inches from the travel agent. Carlo could now see what hung on the chain around Etan's neck. A rooster claw. He also noticed Etan's one green eye.

"The Devil's Bible," Etan said. "Know of it?"

Immediately Carlo nodded. No sense in lying. Lying got you killed.

"Good," Etan said. "That's the part of medieval history I want to talk about. Now, let's jump to recent history. In your capacity as a travel agent, did you or did you not move something related to the Devil's Bible? Eight missing pages, say?"

"Yes, the Black Pages," Carlo said. "I used my source to get them into the United States two days ago."

Etan did not let his disappointment show; not a single tic. He had hoped the pages were still in France. "Who is your source?" he asked.

Carlo didn't hesitate: "Arnaud Tottone."

"Tottone, Tottone... The French ambassador to America?"

"He doesn't have to go through customs," Carlo said. "I give him the merchandise. He gets it into the country, no problem."

"Very good," Etan said, smiling pleasantly. He knew from experience that Carlo would be more forthcoming if he believed he would live. "Okay, last question: do you know who Arnaud Tottone sold the merchandise to?"

"No, I have no idea. Samier paid me my fee and I made the transfer—that's it. That's all I did. I have no idea who he's selling the artifact to. And that's the truth, I swear!"

Etan nodded. He disappeared again into the dark part of the room, but this time he continued to talk to Carlo. "I know you have been involved in this trade for two decades. And I know you have become a student of history like I have. I can't tell you how much I respect that about you, Carlo. So I'm curious: do you know anything about Mesopotamia?"

Tears began to stream down the travel agent's cheeks. He wouldn't survive this. Neumann and Droeger hadn't, and obviously *they* had told the truth about Carlo. "No, I don't. I don't know much about it," he said.

"Well, until recently, historians believed the royal palace attendants willingly ingested poison to join their king and queen in death..."

Etan fell silent. Carlo had the uncanny feeling that he'd moved. He glanced around the basement, straining against the duct tape.

Candlelight and shadow danced around the concrete space. One of the shades seemed darker, and stood very still; Carlo kept his eye on it—and jumped when Etan appeared behind him.

"But it wasn't poison," Etan said, a whisper above a whisper. "They know that now. Turns out these royal handmaidens and warriors were sacrificed with an instrument driven into their heads. A very sharp instrument... like a pike."

"Please..." Carlo said.

"And I will point out to you that this kind of sacrifice was considered a very honorable death."

"Please... I don't know anything!"

Etan held out his hands to show Carlo a steel pike in one, a large hammer in the other.

The travel agent started to scream.

It interested Etan that the Italian's heavy accent vanished in the scream, the same way the accents of British rock singers vanished when they sang.

He stopped Carlo's screaming when he hammered the steel pike into the middle of his head.

After three blows, he stepped away and admired his handiwork. He picked up one of the skulls from the table and ran his thumb over the engraving in the bone, letting the blood on his hands illuminate the text.

Soon, Carlo's skull would bear the same inscription—the words *Angelum Lucis*, which English Bibles translate as "Angel of Light."

CHAPTER 2

A SECRET SERVICE AGENT SEARCHED the list of White House visitors for their names: Envoy John Wolfenson and his aide, Dr. Colin Fincher.

Before their arrival at the gate, the envoy had addressed the doctor privately. "Remember our conversation."

Dr. Fincher had nodded and said, "Of course, Mr. Envoy. I remember every word."

At their first meeting, Fincher had agreed to never utter the name *Angel of Light* in any setting, under any circumstances. These days it seemed like every square foot of real estate had an eye and an ear.

At the visitor computer, the Secret Service agent said, "You've both been cleared."

He gave each of them a visitor's pass, to be worn around their necks at all times. Color-coded bars alerted security personnel to which areas these visitors could access. Wolfenson and Fincher had been coded for the Oval Office.

The White House towered like some Greek temple with pediment and columns. The stone exterior had stood for two centuries as a symbol of permanence, even though it had been gutted and renewed on the inside.

No amount of security could detect the stranger inhabiting the body of Envoy Wolfenson. In no time at all, his footsteps were echoing down the West Wing colonnade and into the corridor to the Oval Office.

Each White House staffer they encountered stopped whatever they were doing to practically unroll a red carpet at Wolfenson's feet. Even one of the chief advisors to the President broke off a conversation with a head of state to shake the envoy's hand.

As they entered the secretary's tiny office and lined up in front of the desk, Fincher caught the envoy staring at his reflection in the bureau mirror. Initially, the Angel of Light had expressed regret that he hadn't chosen a better-looking man. "It's not that John Wolfenson isn't attractive," he had told Fincher. "He most certainly is. But if he were devastatingly handsome, and more physically fit... well, the task at hand would be so much easier to accomplish."

"But," the envoy had also said, "I cannot complain. Together, John and I have more than enough charisma that I won't need my bag of tricks."

Fincher knew this was true. He had researched Envoy John Wolfenson tirelessly before the attack on his life. At any point in the last five years, John could have cashed in his blue chips and spent the rest of his life chasing women and drinking martinis. He had climbed political ladders instead; climbed so high that being voted chairman of the Tri-lateral Commission for another term sounded beneath him.

Usually, accomplished politicians had to wash their hands and suits of mud, and of soot from burning bridges. John had made quite the exception of himself.

He had started as chairman of the Free Trade Commission, and then worked for two years as an advisor to the Secretary of State. His success in that capacity put his name at the top of the list when the President, previous to the incumbent, had gone fishing for the Quartet's new Special Envoy to the Middle East.

From what Fincher could gather, things hadn't come easy for John in international politics. If one of his projects failed, he and his teams couldn't just switch plans like at his old investment firm.

Nevertheless, John rose to the challenge with the enthusiasm and purpose of someone destined for greatness—all while maintaining as many bridges as possible.

Attempting peace in the Middle East had been a brilliant move. Even if he had failed, everyone would have considered it a valiant effort, perhaps one to rival the many efforts before it: the Oslo Accords; the Peace Summit at Camp David.

But John had accomplished the impossible, martyr and savior of the Middle East—and both in the same day.

From her desk, the President's secretary greeted Wolfenson more warmly than she greeted Dr. Fincher. "Good morning, gentlemen. The President is expecting you."

Their Secret Service guide opened the door to the Oval Office. At that moment, standing at the threshold of the world's greatest corridor of power, Dr. Fincher tried to envision what was going through the envoy's mind. He certainly must have felt that all of his plans, some of them thousands of years in the making, had finally been validated.

The Angel of Light entered the Oval Office.

The President of the United States sat behind his desk, the HMS Resolute, which many presidents had used before him. He stood up to be grandly lit by the windows facing the South Lawn. A staff photographer snapped pictures as the Commander in Chief straightened his suit and moved to greet his guest.

"John, great to see you."

"Mr. President." The envoy's footsteps fell softly on the oval rug and its presidential seal. The modesty panel on the Resolute, installed after a request by FDR, bore a similar symbol—except *its* eagle faced the arrows of war.

The room reminded Dr. Fincher of US currency: the minting of coins, the rich and multilayered detail of bills. Scallop shells crowned the recessed shelving and windows. Sunlight featured prominently, glazing the plates on the shelves, turning the glass of paintings into mirrors, so instead of cold pastorals and earthly delights, Fincher glimpsed the Angel of Light, who shined.

"Thank you for having me here at the White House," Wolfenson said to the President.

They shook hands, and a second later the President's other hand joined in.

Dr. Fincher wondered how long the display of affection would last. Probably no longer than the President's campaign promises after the election.

A few more flashes and the photographer left.

The envoy introduced Dr. Fincher, who was surprised to learn that the leader of their country had soft hands.

The President motioned to the sitting area near the fireplace. "Please, why don't you both have a seat? Can I get you anything to drink? Coffee?"

A cup already steamed on the little table between the couches.

"No thanks, Mr. President," the envoy said, taking a seat opposite the cup. "We just came from breakfast."

As Dr. Fincher moved to sit beside Wolfenson, he noticed that the President was staring at the envoy's neck—at the pink and jagged scar partially hidden by his collar.

The President sat down in front of his cup, still smiling; Fincher didn't buy it. Perhaps the whole meeting was being recorded. It wouldn't be the first time in the Oval Office. And the doctor could think of no other reason for the warm reception.

After his election, the President had kept Wolfenson on as the envoy for an additional year, or until his peace process lost momentum; he never truly believed Wolfenson was capable of convincing six different Arab countries to sign a wide-range, seven-year peace treaty with Israel. And of course the President could never have foreseen that the envoy would end up an international celebrity after surviving a brutal assassination attempt.

The President said, "So, John, tell me: how many times did you have to rehearse for the TV show last night? You were hysterical."

"Mr. President, you're too kind Surely you could tell my voice was trembling worse than my hands. And that was *after* I made them rewrite two of their jokes."

"I'm serious, you came off quite well. Come up with some magic tricks and they'll have you on every week."

"No," Wolfenson said, "one time on the show was plenty. Besides, it was Patricia's idea. She's the real fan. Want to hear the first thing she asked me after the show?"

The President nodded as if he were listening, then leaned forward to grab his coffee.

"She wanted to know what the host said to me right before the commercial break. When the music started to play."

The President's hand paused halfway to his coffee mug. He arched an eyebrow, clearly as curious about the exchange as Patricia had been.

Wolfenson satisfied his curiosity: "He asked if I would show him my scar."

The President glanced at Wolfenson's neck. "What did you do, John?"

The envoy smiled. "I showed him my scar. This one, under my chin—the one I got as a teenager when I fell off my skateboard."

"Hah!" The President seemed genuinely amused. He picked up his coffee and took a sip.

"Mr. President, I'm curious," Wolfenson said. "You were on his show..."

"Yes, I was. Twice during the campaign."

"If you don't mind me asking, what did the host say to you when the show was going to a commercial break?"

The President smiled as he recalled the incident. "He leaned in and told me, 'I'm not a registered voter, but if I was, I would be voting for you.'"

Both Dr. Fincher and Wolfenson laughed.

The President certainly seemed pleased by their reaction, but as he sipped his coffee his demeanor once again turned serious. "Coincidently, John, that story is the perfect segue into the problem with our relationship." He set his cup on the table and said, "I don't think you voted for me."

The Angel of Light sat in silence. It crossed Fincher's mind that the President had caught him off-guard, but, no, the envoy had calculated exactly how long to pause.

Wolfenson said, "You're right, Mr. President. I didn't vote for you."

The President's eyebrows jumped a little in surprise. Fincher believed he wasn't reacting to the answer, but to its candor.

"But two years from now, when you run for a second term, Mr. President, I will not only vote for you, I will campaign for you."

Slowly, a grin spread across the President's face. Dr. Fincher believed it was the Commander in Chief's first genuine smile since he and the envoy had entered the Oval Office.

———

FINCHER AND WOLFENSON FOLLOWED the Secret Service agent back to the north portico of the White House. Across the North Lawn, beyond the fountain, a uniformed officer patrolled the iron fence. Nearly two dozen protestors picketed just on the other side, all along Pennsylvania Avenue.

Everything appeared to have gone well. They had left the President of the United States thoroughly convinced that the envoy's future exploits would never overshadow the White House's own efforts in foreign policy. In exchange, the White House would not interfere with

Wolfenson's business ventures. The President even went so far as to support the envoy's efforts wherever they shared common ground.

With cunning, cleverness, and charisma the Angel of Light had just secured backing from the greatest superpower on Earth. As their Town Car passed through the main gate of the White House, Dr. Fincher smiled at the protestors marching along the White House fence. They were picketing the President's economic policy, his foreign policy, his social agenda—basically all of his actions since he took office. A majority vote had declared him the winner of the election, but the results certainly didn't silence the parts of the country that couldn't stand the man.

One of the protesters carried a sign that read, "The Antichrist is in the Oval Office."

The envoy saw the sign and laughed. "It's tempting to yell out the window that he's wrong: the Antichrist just *left* the Oval Office."

Dr. Fincher took the opportunity to laugh. So rarely did the envoy joke.

CHAPTER 3

"AND WITH THE ENERGY from your new diet of animal flesh, you might have some free time for something more useful. Like thinking. And hunting. And having sex."

Jenna Grant moved closer to the studio microphone for emphasis. "So *that*, in a nutshell, is the basic day-to-day life if you were *Australopithecus africanus*, our common ancestor. I hope you think about this diet as you eat your English breakfast of..." Jenna turned to her radio co-host, Raymond Chappell, who sat at the microphone opposite hers. "Raymond, help me out. What do you folks eat here in this country for breakfast?"

"Kippers and crumpet," Raymond said.

Jenna grimaced. "Yes, kippers and crumpet. A diet of scavenged meat and savannah leaves is sounding better and better."

The producer and engineer of the show, Callie Woodward, motioned to Jenna and Raymond that they only had thirty seconds left.

Jenna nodded and said, "Time to talk about what's in store next week. We've got a great show planned, including an exciting segment on the ancient drawings I researched in Malta. These cave paintings should provoke some interesting conspiracy theories about what might have happened to one of the thriving tribes in the area."

"And," Raymond said, "we'll talk about how Jenna and I got into an argument over what really happened to the tribe."

He and Jenna met eyes, and by his grin she knew instantly that they were improvising.

"Now, now, Raymond, I wouldn't call it an argument."

"Yes, more like a steel cage death match over at Gerry's Pub."

They both laughed to sell the joke, and then Jenna lowered her voice to a husky whisper for her audience, but kept her eyes on Raymond. "All that and much, much more when you join us next week for *Archeology: Stripped and Exposed*."

The show's theme music came on, and Callie used her fingers to count them out. Ten seconds later, they were off the air.

Jenna took off her headphones, and she and Raymond bumped fists, chuckling, which they did after each show.

Archeology: Stripped and Exposed, despite its provocative title, originally had appealed to hardcore science enthusiasts. But when management figured out that hardcore science enthusiasts comprised a very small niche, they decided to hire a female co-host. "To add spice," as one of the managers had put it. Or, according to the show's original host, Bob Coben, "To tart up my show."

Jenna had no illusions why they had hired her. Sure, she had a PhD in archeology, but so did everyone else who had applied for the job. Management brought her on because she looked as young and cute as she sounded over the air. Her hiring wasn't a unanimous decision: the president of sales had pointed out that she lacked a British accent; unlike the hosts of the other radio science shows, she was American. But she ended up getting the job anyway.

At first, Jenna hadn't understood why sex appeal mattered in radio. She hadn't known about promotion. But she learned about it quickly her first month on the job. She attended three fairs, six college orientations, and two TV talk shows, then panicked when she realized photographs of these events had been published online and in print—she had been caught wearing the same three outfits from her limited wardrobe.

"See you at Gerry's?" Raymond asked her. Ever since their first show, they had met with Callie at a pub near the university. They usually discussed what had gone wrong that night and what they could do better, but they also simply relaxed and had drinks.

"Yeah, absolutely," Jenna said. "I'll meet you guys there after I've made a few calls."

At her desk, she dialed her mother in the States, but got her voicemail. Typical these days. And not just because of the time difference between Cambridge and Virginia; her mother recently had hip surgery and required round-the-clock care.

"Mom, hope you're well," Jenna said. "Just got off the air and am leaving to have a drink. I'll call you tomorrow."

She hung up and thought about touching base with her brother Neal, who lived in Georgetown, D.C. They hadn't talked in over a month because Jenna had been travelling and working on digs in Jordan and

Malta. However, Neal had sent a few email updates regarding their mother's health.

Jenna decided not to call. It was almost the end of the workday in his corner of the world.

At Gerry's Pub, she ordered a cosmopolitan, which the waitress served with a smirk. It raised eyebrows to order anything other than pints of beer.

"Cheers," Callie said, toasting with Raymond and Jenna. "To another fabulous show."

Callie went on and on about the live phone interview with Raymond's mother, who had told a great story about Raymond unearthing his first fossil while cleaning out her garage. "It's exactly the kind of personal touch that management wants to see," she said.

"I didn't hog the show, did I?" Jenna asked.

"No, we got a fair share of both of you," Callie replied, but Jenna really wanted Raymond's reaction. His athletic build and dirty-blond hair attracted a sizeable female audience who normally wouldn't care about cave drawings or ancient artifacts, or anything Jenna had to say. That's why station management had hired Raymond as Jenna's co-host. Poor Bob Coben's contract was never renewed. Jenna had heard that when Bob first met Raymond, he took one look at the new co-host and said, "The two tarts have taken over my show." At least Jenna didn't end up feeling resented because she was female.

"I actually thought it was the perfect balance between listening to your sexy voice and me prattling on," Raymond said. He winked and took a big gulp of beer.

Raymond's English accent often distracted Jenna from whatever he was saying because he sounded as if he were singing. When she first arrived in England to undertake her masters at Cambridge, she told her mother that being murdered by an Englishman wouldn't be half bad. At least his death threats would sound polite.

After Callie finished discussing the broadcast, Raymond ordered another round of drinks.

"So," he said to Jenna, "are we ready to see who'll pay the bill?"

Jenna smiled and leaned forward. Raymond once told her she looked like a giddy schoolgirl whenever they were about to play the game, and she guessed she kind of felt like one.

They had invented it one night after an on-air discussion about some Roman coins a listener had mailed in. Raymond believed the coins to be authentic, but Jenna didn't buy it. A microscope at one of the college laboratories settled the matter. Having been proven wrong, Raymond insisted on buying drinks for Jenna and Callie.

And thus began their weekly challenge of "Spot the Fake." Raymond and Jenna took turns bringing to the pub different artifacts, such as Greek Tanagra figurines, which the other would then have to authenticate or judge as fake. Last month, Jenna especially had some fun challenging Raymond with an authentic twenty-first century Prada handbag and a fake one she'd bought on a street corner back in the United States. Switching from ancient artifacts to modern design accessories didn't change the outcome—Raymond ended up picking up the tab for all the drinks that night. But Jenna made sure he didn't leave the pub without a consolation prize: she gave him the faux Prada, which he then gave to his sister as a birthday gift. Apparently his sister had the same eye for authenticity as he did, because she strutted around Manchester, showing off her expensive new bag.

"So you say one of your specialties is paleography?" Raymond asked Jenna with a sly grin.

"No," she said, "it's my *special* specialty."

"Right. So here's the challenge." From his backpack, Raymond produced a legal-sized photocopy of a vellum page and laid it on the table in front of her. "This is a document supposedly written anywhere from the fourteenth to the fifteenth century. Your challenge, if you choose to accept, is to tell me whether it's authentic or a forgery... and why."

Jenna couldn't stop grinning. After her BS in archeology, she did her graduate work in paleography at Cambridge. Raymond wasn't just testing her expertise in ancient texts; he was indulging her love of them.

She picked up the photocopied vellum and focused.

Greek lettering. Definitely from a reed and not a pen, evidenced by the thickness. Forty-six lines from the New Testament—John 3:2, Matthew 14:12, and a phrase from Luke 7:47-50. Not hard to translate for someone who knew Greek, Hebrew and Latin.

She raised her drink to her lips, but the glass was empty. She'd been studying and translating longer than she realized.

"Well?" Raymond asked. He and Callie both smiled in anticipation.

Jenna said, "Raymond, my dear boy. This is not a very clever item somebody has cooked up."

He arched an eyebrow, as if in amusement, but she knew it was a trick to make her doubt her conviction. "Why, Jenna, are you accusing them of forgery?"

"That's exactly what I'm accusing them of. Order me another drink and I'll tell you why."

"No problem. Because this week I think you'll be the one paying."

Raymond motioned to the waitress for another round as Callie leaned in for a look at the photocopy.

"First off," Jenna said, "look at the lines of text. They're all uneven."

Callie nodded.

"That's because the page hasn't been ruled with an awl, so there aren't any horizontal lines or grooves to help the medieval scribe line up the letters. The forger must have figured a modern ruler would look too obvious, but he clearly didn't know they had ways of keeping their text straight even in the fourteenth and fifteenth century."

She glanced at Raymond, and the look on his face made her grin all over again. "Second," she said, "see how the paragraphs of text are indented?"

"Yes," Callie said, "I can see that."

"Well, indenting paragraphs is a modern fabrication, not a medieval one. And look: this word here..." She pointed it out on the legal-sized page. "It's Greek for *Heaven*. Except back then, they didn't write out words like *Heaven* or *God*. They contracted them and put a horizontal bar across the top, sort of like the apostrophe in *can't*, or... more like an abbreviation."

Raymond, shaking his head, pulled out his wallet and started to count how many pounds he actually had on him.

"Lastly," Jenna said, just to show off, "let's look at this part of the text. John 3:2. It uses the phrase 'to Jesus.' That's a modern translation. The more accurate phrase would be 'to him,' which would have been more consistent with manuscripts of this age. And I won't even go into how the document drops John's double amen."

She ran out of breath on the last few words and finally stopped to catch it.

The waitress appeared with the next round of drinks.

"I'll be taking the check tonight," Raymond told her.

Callie, who had been too engrossed to touch her drink, turned to Jenna. "Girl, if I were gay, I'd be all over your smart, sexy ass right now."

"Oh, that wouldn't be possible," Raymond said, smiling despite his bitter tone. "Our girl here doesn't date those with whom she works."

Months ago Jenna had put a stop to Raymond's initial hints that they should go on a date. "This is business," she had said. "Not pleasure. When the two get mixed up, it oftentimes ends up a threesome— business, pleasure... lawsuit."

"Yes, I hear you Americans can be very litigious," Raymond had said. "But what if we end up not working together? Who knows? I could get fired."

As it turned out, Raymond performed as well as Jenna did on the air, so the subject never came up again.

Jenna's cell phone rang, blessedly. She checked the caller ID. "Sorry, I need to get this," she said, even as she was flipping open the phone and pressing it to her ear. "Hello—Neal?"

"Hey, sis. I'm probably disturbing you, I know."

"Is everything all right? Where are you?"

"Listen, Mom's fine."

Jenna felt the muscles in her back loosen a little.

"Well," Neal said, "she did fire one of the nurses working the overnight shift in her house. But that's not why I called. I need your help."

"Neal, hold on a second. I can barely hear you." Jenna made her way out to the street, where it was much quieter.

"Okay, what's going on?" she asked him. "Are you all right?"

"Absolutely. I'm doing just fine Better than fine. I just need you to help me with something."

"Help with what? Something here across the pond?"

"No, not really," Neal said. "I need you to come to D.C."

Jenna heard something in his voice, as if more than just an ocean separated them.

Three men emerged from the pub, laughing and shouting and kicking their mate's hat like a football. Jenna moved down the pavement a dozen feet.

"D.C.?" Jenna asked. "When?"

"I've booked you a redeye flight. It leaves tonight."

"That's crazy. I can't just pick up and leave, Neal. I've got a job. I've got a cat. I—"

"I thought you got rid of the cat."

"Yeah, he's staying with a neighbor most of the time. I was allergic, okay?"

"Look, I know I'm asking a lot," Neal said, "but I need you to come back and put some of that higher education into action."

Jenna feared this day would come. Neal had paid for her graduate school, and had arranged for her first two jobs: a research project at the Smithsonian, and, one year later, the Aquincum dig in Budapest. She had started calling him the Octopus because he seemed to have tentacles touching everyone in archeology.

Jenna hated not paying her own way, and she certainly didn't want to owe anyone, even her brother. A year ago she tried to pay him back, but he refused, telling her it wasn't a loan, it was a gift. Apparently on some gifts, you can charge interest.

"I don't understand," Jenna said. "Do you need me to consult on a project you're involved in, or... ?"

"Look, I can't talk about it on the phone. But you know I wouldn't ask you to fly out here if this wasn't important to me. I've emailed you the ticket information. You'll be here for less than forty-eight hours, and gone before you know it."

"What sort of project are you working on?" she asked.

"It's not really a project. It's... a business deal. But I don't want to talk about it on the phone. And, by the way, don't mention the reason for your trip to anyone."

"Mention what? I don't know what I'll be doing."

"Oh, this is coming off way too mysterioso," Neal said. "I just need you to authenticate something for me, that's all. Something from the thirteenth century. I assure you, it's totally in your wheelhouse. So bring whatever you'll need to conduct some rudimentary tests."

"Will I have time to prepare?" Jenna asked. It wasn't really the question she wanted him to answer, but she asked it anyway.

"Yes, yes, after you get to your hotel I'll give you some background and time to prepare."

"What's wrong with your guest room?"

Neal said, "Can't do it this time. I have some construction guys at the house, so I've booked you a room at a nice hotel. It's kind of a surprise. You'll see. All the details are in an email I'll be sending you. Oh, and here's the best part—I'm giving you some... let's call it travelling money. Some around-the-world traveling money. For helping me out. Deal?"

"You're sure there's no way this can wait?"

"Just be on the flight, okay, sis?"

Nothing ever seemed to ruffle Neal's Brooks Brothers suit. And yet here he was, practically reaching through the phone lines with his octopus arms and shoving her to the airport.

"Will I be meeting you at the terminal?" she asked. "Or catching a cab?"

"All the details are in the email. Look, I got to go."

Neal hung up.

Jenna was shocked. "I love you too," she said.

CHAPTER 4

GEORGE WYATT STARED at the newly erected headstone, then consulted his watch.

Twenty minutes had passed since his call to the cemetery's office. Twenty infinite minutes. And he had counted each one on the black minute hand, had witnessed the red second hand killing time.

They say the mind kicks into slow motion right before an accident, the body's little trick to aid quick and proper reaction. They also say the body can get stuck in a flight-or-flight response, which leads to panic attacks. George's body had done something similar, only it had stuck in slow motion. The minute people opened their mouths, he knew exactly how trite their condolences would be, and yet he had to hear them out.

On the street adjacent to the burial plot, a black car pulled up. Finally.

Hal Larson, the cemetery representative, tried for poise as he hurried up the grassy knoll.

"Mr. Wyatt," he said, catching his breath. "You called our office with a complaint?"

"Yes," George said, "you misspelled it."

"I'm sorry? Can you—"

"Her name. You misspelled it."

Larson studied the headstone, dabbing at his sweaty brow with a handkerchief. "It says Carrie Wyatt. That's not correct?"

"I told you. She spells it without an *e*."

Larson failed to hide the briefest skeptical frown as he withdrew a pocket notebook from inside his suit. He flipped through several pages, then stopped somewhere near the end. He blushed.

"Mr. Wyatt..." he said, slowly closing the notebook before meeting George's eyes. "In the twenty years I've worked at Lullaby Hills, a mistake of this kind has never occurred."

George said, "That would be so meaningful to me... if I were from the Better Business Bureau. But I'm just a husband trying to bury his wife."

"Please, our humblest apologies. I assure you, we'll..."

Larson's mouth began to move slower than the minute hand on George's watch. So instead of saying something he would regret, George walked off down the hill.

———

HE STARED OUT AT THE POTOMAC RIVER as the train crossed into Washington D.C. The distant buildings reminded him of neoclassical mausoleums and sepulchers; the Washington Monument stood like an obelisk in a graveyard.

Though the early morning rush hour had passed, people filled the train. George had been lucky enough to get a seat in the Quiet Car, just behind the locomotive. Lucky or cursed, because now he could hear his own thoughts.

Running parallel to the Virginia Railway, a bright blue car crossed the Memorial Bridge. It was a pretty common little car. Great fuel economy. World-class airbags. And this one was the same blue as Carri's.

Whenever they travelled together, Carri forced George to drive her around because she claimed to be a crazy woman driver. It made him laugh that she would stereotype herself. But he didn't mind being her chauffer. In fact he kind of enjoyed it.

He'd been the one behind the wheel that day after shopping. They shouldn't have gone out, he knew that now. The city had been covered in a snowfall from hell, lit merrily with Christmas lights. But they needed a few last-minute presents, so off they went.

Carri sat in the passenger seat, wearing her Washington Redskins cap and taking pictures of the view. "This is beautiful. Like a whole city made out of snow." She lowered the camera and said, "Pull over so I can get some good shots."

"No way," George replied. "You'll freeze your caboose off."

"Well then, turn up the heater." She smiled and rolled down her power window, then leaned out with her camera. But not before setting her ball cap safely in the center console; he would end up burying her with it.

"Carri, get back in here. It's cold."

She unbuckled her seatbelt and leaned out even farther for the view. "Sometimes you got to suffer for your art."

"Hey, it's not *my* art," George said, turning to watch her. "Why should I be the one to suffer—"

Brake lights flashed in front of him. He tried to stop.

Their car skated gracefully in slow motion, so that each snowflake hung suspended in midair. And then they crashed into a snow bank.

The car's world-class airbags deployed, even though Carri's weight no longer activated the passenger seat.

To this day, George still couldn't remember climbing out of the car, but apparently he had. A few yards away he found his wife, whose blood had begun to pool and steam like her breath. If she had landed anywhere else, drifts of snow would have cushioned her. But because of some cosmic joke, her body ended up on a small section of blacktop recently shoveled. And the punch line turned out to be the misspelling on her grave.

In the Quiet Car, signs prohibited cell phones but encouraged whispering. George had been rapping his knuckles on the window without even realizing it—until he was shushed by a fellow passenger. Everyone else looked away, suddenly pretending they were too polite to stare.

George lowered his arm like an hour hand. No sooner did he begin keeping time with his foot.

CHAPTER 5

FINCHER TOLD THE SECRETARY to hold all calls: their boss had just struck a lucrative deal. Then he let himself into the tenth floor conference room. Quietly, Fincher shut the door behind him because he didn't want to disturb the image in front of him.

Envoy John Wolfenson stood at the wall of glass overlooking Washington D.C., which must have looked like New Rome to eyes that old. The petty political battles that dominated the landscape must have only amused him.

"So, did I live up to your expectations?" Wolfenson asked.

"Envoy, sir, you continue to exceed them. You impressed even their lawyer."

The position of Envoy to the Quartet paid no income, except for tax dollars from the United States, Russia, and the European Union. The monies covered personal expenses and paid off dedicated staff. The real money came from Wolfenson Enterprises, his consulting firm. But to say that his political position didn't have financial rewards would have been naïve.

The envoy had just closed a multi-million-dollar deal to represent a Milwaukee-based grocery chain which was branching out into the Middle East.

"And this is just the opening act," Fincher said. He took his notebook from his jacket and consulted their agenda. "I have even higher expectations for the deal with J.M. Morgan—"

"What time are they expecting us?"

"Three o'clock. And yet what we could potentially get from J.M. Morgan is a drop in the bucket compared to what I believe Prince Haddaj Al-Aziz will be offering for your services. A deal with him gets us that much closer to working with the entire family, which should provide a windfall in the coming years—"

"We don't have years," the envoy said, still staring out the window. "The Landlord knows I'm here."

Landlord. The envoy's euphemism for God. The conference room was regularly swept for bugs, so privacy wasn't the reason Wolfenson spoke in code. Since their first meeting weeks ago in Jerusalem's Balshem Medical Center, Dr. Fincher had become aware that Wolfenson refused to use any reference to God other than "Landlord."

"I do understand, Mr. Envoy. Perhaps if I knew more about what we'll be up against..."

"Doctor, when I have more information, I promise you I won't be shy about sharing. But one of the few things I cannot do is predict my own future. However, I will predict this..." Wolfenson turned from the window and said, "We must keep pressing forward. Because when the

Landlord does eventually act, it will only make it harder for our plan to succeed."

Fincher took a seat at the conference table. "We have some time before our meeting with J.M. Morgan." he said, flipping to another page in his notebook. "Shall we discuss your wife?"

Wolfenson nodded and took the chair across from him. "I fear she still suspects me."

Fincher felt the briefest twinge in his gut. "What? Has she said something?"

"No. But faces don't lie. They twitch, they tell. And Patricia, when she looks at me... it's as if she knows."

"Have you stuck to John's previous dietary habits?" Fincher asked.

"As best I can. We've gone to several restaurants in the past few weeks, places we've been to before. The waiters all insisted that I have my usual, uh... dead animal dish. I found it impossible to keep down."

"And what was Patricia's reaction?" Fincher asked.

"She actually laughed when I said I was thinking of becoming a vegetarian."

"Did you tell her you're trying to eat healthier since the attack?"

"Yes, for all it's worth."

"And the alcohol," Fincher said, "how are you coping with that?"

"I told her my doctor forbade any alcohol during my recuperation. But now that I've recovered, she's wondering why my desire for vodka martinis hasn't recovered as well."

"Perhaps you could incorporate at least a single drink per night as part of your routine," Fincher suggested.

"I would rather not. I know it's difficult to understand, doctor, but sustaining this possession is a delicate matter. Besides, the main problem isn't dietary. Prior to my arrival, I believe John and Patricia's relationship endured more than its fair share of acrimony. And therein lies the issue. The behavior, habits, and routines of one you resent are oftentimes more closely observed than those of someone you love."

"I see."

"Before our trip to the White House, she said she might go to her therapist."

"The one she saw after your son's death?"

"Yes."

"I suggest you let her go."

"I felt like I had no choice."

"So it's already done."

"Yes, of course."

Dr. Fincher nodded and flipped through a few pages. "Oh, I meant to ask you.... What about your dreams? Anything different?"

"No. And I don't expect them to be. During my other possessions, I always had their dreams. John is no different."

Dr. Fincher recorded the envoy's answer in a sort of encryption, and then tucked the notebook back into his jacket. He leaned across the conference table to press the intercom button.

"Clara," he said to the secretary, "I think we'll have lunch now..."

"Sorry, Clara," Wolfenson interrupted, "change of plans. We'll be going out for lunch."

Dr. Fincher clicked off the intercom.

"I've arranged a meeting with Carl."

Fincher waited for Wolfenson to elaborate, but the envoy's silence forced him to nod, as if he understood. He clicked on the intercom again. "Clara, can you call for our car? Thanks."

———

THEY TOOK A TOWN CAR TO THE OVAL ROOM, a restaurant near the U.S. Chamber of Commerce. The driver parked at one of the meters along Connecticut Avenue, where on the sidewalk, Carl Saracen waited. His tousled, peppered white hair and deeply tanned face set him apart from the pale, portly Washingtonians standing nearby.

Fincher started to open his door, but Wolfenson laid a hand on his shoulder.

"Please, Colin, if you don't mind, I wish to see Carl alone."

Fincher studied the envoy for a moment, but saw only kindness and charm in the lines around his mouth and eyes. "Of course," he said, realizing how bald his suspicions must have been. "Do what you must."

"Thank you." Wolfenson squeezed Fincher's shoulder and then got out. Before the car door shut, Fincher locked eyes with Carl Saracen, who didn't look surprised that Fincher wouldn't be joining them for lunch.

From behind the Lincoln's tinted windows, the doctor watched the envoy shake Carl's hand, and squeeze his shoulder too. He watched the hostess seat the two men on the patio, under a green umbrella. And then for some time he lost sight of them as restaurant patrons crowded around to get the envoy's autograph or a photo, or at least to shake his hand.

———

AFTER LUNCH, DR. FINCHER and Wolfenson attended the meeting at J.M. Morgan. Everyone in the room understood how much money was moving around the Middle East. "And it would be a shame if J.M. Morgan wasn't managing it," Wolfenson said.

After they settled the envoy's consulting fee, everyone shook hands. Fincher knew how reassuring Wolfenson's handshake could be: with just the right amount of pump and pressure, and nothing to prove.

The deal was all but closed. The lawyers only had to amend the contract, and then deliver signature copies to both parties before the end of the week.

On their way to the envoy's townhouse in Dupont Circle, Wolfenson and Dr. Fincher sat opposite each other in the back of the Town Car. The envoy stared out the window, his eyes reflecting city lights. Fincher sat in the dark.

In moments like this, the doctor tried to steal long looks at the envoy. But not too long; he never wanted Wolfenson to feel like one of his test subjects.

"Doctor," the envoy said, "if you have something on your mind, speak it. No secrets here."

Fincher blushed; to have been so easily read, and without eye contact. He said, "I've hesitated to ask you... the things I've longed to know."

"Yes, your restraint is commendable. But please..." Wolfenson, glowing dimly in the passing lights, met the doctor's eyes. "Ask me anything you want."

"You've been here before," he said, "obviously."

"Hmm, less than you would think," Wolfenson replied. "We have a deal, the Landlord and I. Any direct intervention on my part will be met with retribution. So I've kept my physical visits here to an absolute minimum."

When Fincher said nothing more, Wolfenson cocked an eyebrow. "So that's it? That's the question at the top of your list?"

"No. I guess what I would most like to ask is... what happened? Between you and... the Landlord?"

"The fall—is that what you are asking about?"

Fincher wasn't sure whether Wolfenson could see him nodding in the dark, but it didn't matter because the envoy answered anyway.

"As I said, I have visited this sad planet before. And on each occasion I possessed a human being. I did so because I wanted to understand what it felt like to be one of his favored creatures. Each time, the experience was the same: a short, empty existence full of abuse and debasement, and never enough knowledge to escape a life of folly.

"It has always been that way. And always will be. From the very beginning, the Landlord made a mistake... a mistake that to this day he refuses to admit."

Fincher thought he knew the mistake to which Wolfenson was referring, but didn't want to interrupt for clarification now that he had him talking.

"When we were still on speaking terms, I told the Landlord that all of you would love to live up to his expectations, but that you would fail... and continue to fail. As I'm sure you'll agree, I proved more than prophetic. After a certain point, I could not stand to watch your pointless suffering any longer. So I did something about it. And I wasn't the only one. But our... *insurrection* failed. And we were punished. And that, dear doctor, brings us to current events.

"So, you see, my falling out with him was because I loved you... all of you. And I still do. That is why I'm here."

CHAPTER 6

JENNA AWOKE TO A PHONE CALL in her hotel room in D.C. It was her brother, Neal.

"I trust you made it all right?" he asked.

Jenna grunted, only half-awake.

"Great," Neal said. "Look, I'm here in the lobby. Can you come down and we'll get this ball rolling? I'm on a schedule."

Jenna said yeah and hung up, then groaned into her pillow. She had slept no more than a few minutes on the flight from London, too troubled and excited by Neal's *mysterioso* project.

Before going downstairs to meet him, she went into the bathroom to freshen up. She took one look at the kink in her hair and thought, *Who cares?* This wasn't a promotional event for the show. It was her brother.

As per Neal's instructions, Jenna hadn't mentioned the purpose of her vacation to anyone, but she did tell her co-workers where she would be. She took a second to text Raymond, so she could brag: her brother had booked her a room two blocks from the White House in the Willard InterContinental.

When Neal and Jenna were kids, their mother had taken them on a tour of D.C., and Jenna, upon first stepping foot into The Willard, had said, "Mom, can we stay here? Please?" She knew that the word *please* showed off her missing front teeth, which grownups found irresistible. Not so irresistible as to afford the Willard, however. Later, Neal had asked her why she'd wanted to stay there, and she told him the ghost story: that with every breath, you could be inhaling the last breath of someone famous, some great historical figure; those odds increased when you spent the night at one of their old haunts. Neal, of course, had called her a freak.

As Jenna was leaving her room, Raymond answered her message. He used his smartphone as an alarm clock, so even if he was sleeping, he tended to answer texts. *Send me pics!* he said.

Since her childhood tour, the lobby of the hotel had been renovated and was new all over again. Jenna had been too tired on her way in from Reagan National to properly admire it, so she took a good look now as she descended the grand staircase. The various surfaces of wood, stone, and ornamentation seemed marbled, filigreed, or minted subtly with gold. Chandeliers hung in globes of pure light.

She stopped about halfway down to take a picture of the coffered ceiling, which, in panels of gold leaf, featured the seal of every U.S. state. She sent it on to Raymond.

Jenna spotted her brother in the center of the lobby, where chairs and fronds and little tables had been set around massive pillars of faux marble. At least she *thought* it was her brother; he stood looking toward the front entrance, so Jenna couldn't see his face. The man certainly had Neal's posture: very sure of his footing, yet casual enough to rest his hands in his pockets.

"Neal!" Jenna said.

He turned, and she caught him in a tight, warm hug.

"I can't believe you put me up at The Willard!"

He chuckled and then let her go. "Glad you like your surprise. You see, I *was* listening to you when we were kids."

Jenna's smile faded as she got a good look at him. Several small cuts dotted his cheeks and brow. They had scabbed over, but some of them looked like they had originally been serious abrasions.

"Neal, what the hell happened to your face?"

"Maybe the same thing that happened to your hair," he shot back.

"Neal, I'm not kidding..."

"Oh come on, Jenna, it's no big deal. Seriously. I should have said something when it happened, but... you already had *one* family member to worry about."

"So what happened?"

"Oh, just some blonde named Carol stopped short, and I flew off my bike into her back windshield. No big deal."

"Oh my god," she said, ignoring the comment about the blonde. "Did you need stitches?"

"No, don't be ridiculous. I just had some bandages for a few days and that was it. But I did see a lawyer. I'm pretty positive that the driver did it on purpose; she thought I was tailgating her."

Jenna didn't know what to think. First the strange phone call, now this.

"Okay," she said, moving on, "you've got to tell me. Why the heck am I here?"

Neal broke eye contact and turned to the side, motioning with his hand to the lobby. "Don't you want to luxuriate in the scenery first? Beautiful, right? Did you know we get the word *lobbyist* from this exact hotel?"

"Oh God, you're not going to tell the story of Ulysses S. Grant, are you?"

"Why? You know it?"

"Well, actually..." Jenna said, and Neal rolled his eyes. "What?" she asked.

"You said *actually*. You always say that before correcting someone."

She had to admit he was right. She would also muster as much air as she could before the correction, so that she could spit it out as quickly as possible; somehow she thought celerity lessened the offense.

"Actually..." she said, "it is true that Grant smoked his cigars here in the lobby—because his wife didn't let him do it in the White House. And, yes, people did often approach him to curry favor while he was relaxing here..."

"Right." Neal nodded. "Lobbyists."

"But!" Jenna held up a finger, a gesture she'd inherited from their mother. "The term actually originated in Britain where Members of Parliament would gather in the lobbies of the House of Commons— more than two decades before Grant ever became president."

For a second, Neal looked like that little boy who always told on his kid sister for being such a snot. But then he grinned and shook his head. "How do you know all this stuff?"

"The same way I know this hotel has lodged just about every U.S. President since Franklin Pierce."

"And how's that?"

Jenna crossed her arms and gave him a look. "What've you done with my brother?"

"Excuse me?"

"The Neal I know once got in trouble for putting a gummy worm in my library books."

"Oh, right. Bookworm."

"Yeah, right. That's my loving brother. He doesn't even remember me reading about the Willard for days."

"Oh yeah, you *were* quite obsessed. And actually..." He put his hand on her shoulder and started to guide her toward a bar at the back of the hotel. "That's exactly why I called you here. You never accept anything at face value—never have. That's why I knew I could only trust one person with the job."

Jenna smiled and felt a small rush in the pit of her gut. "Then stop keeping me in suspense already and tell me what this is all about."

"Well..." He glanced around, as if someone might be eavesdropping.

As long as Jenna could remember, Neal seemed to have a drink in his hand and a smile on his face. Even when he was a Wall Street broker, raising capital for business ventures and hedge funds, he never showed a single ounce of stress. At least not in front of her. But now his smile was gone, and he didn't even glance at the bar as they passed into the adjacent hallway.

He said, "We need to cover some ground rules first. Rules you need to take very seriously, Jenna."

"Hey, you know I can keep a secret if that's what you need to hear. Mom still doesn't know what you and Debbie Ann Johnson did in her bed." Jenna expected a smile at the very least, but the expression on Neal's face didn't change.

He said, "It's not just that you can't speak to anyone ever about what you see tonight. That goes without saying. I also need you to shut off that inquiring mind of yours and not ask any questions."

Jenna stopped walking and put her hand on her brother's arm, forcing him to face her. "Neal, does someone have you doing something? Something you don't want to do?"

He chuckled, but then must have realized how deep her frown had gotten. "See," he said, "this is why I want to get the rules straight. Sometimes your mind takes you to some crazy places."

Jenna studied him, but couldn't figure him out. The cuts really threw her off. They seemed to make his face stiff, as if maybe it was painful to move it too much. "Okay then. I won't tell anyone about anything that happens tonight. And I won't ask you or anyone else any questions, all right?"

Neal nodded and they started walking again, headed for a set of glass doors that opened up at the back of the hotel.

"Now," Jenna said, "tell me what I've gotten myself into."

Neal held open one of the doors for her, and as she walked through, he leaned in and whispered, "The Codex Gigas. Otherwise known as— *The Devil's Bible.*"

CHAPTER 7

D R. BENJAMIN HARTMAN greeted Patricia Wolfenson in the waiting room. Her handshake was cold. His was gentle and warm.

"It's been awhile," Dr. Hartman said as they made their way into his office. "What's it been, three years?"

"I think so," Patricia said, "yes."

The furniture in his office remained leather-clad and trimmed with cherry wood, but apparently he had been traveling; wooden tikis lined his bookshelf, and a koa carving of Buddha peeked out from behind his desk. Spruce resin incense hung in the air.

The doctor sat in his leather club chair, and Patricia chose the same seat she always did, on the end of the couch farthest from him.

"I was relieved to hear that your husband recovered from the attack," Dr. Hartman said as he settled into the creaking leather.

Patricia nodded. "Thank you for the card, by the way. It was very thoughtful."

"Well, I must admit, I also wanted to remind you that I'm here if you ever need me."

"Well, I guess it worked," Patricia said.

Her reaction reminded Dr. Hartman of the old Patricia, who, for nearly a year after her son's death, still spent her worst days in bed; the Patricia who believed her relatives and friends were pushing her to move on. She had cut herself off from her family, had simply stopped calling them. And she also had stopped talking to her husband, John. She resented him for going back to work too soon, as if nothing had happened.

John had come to see Dr. Hartman a few times for couples therapy, and he claimed to have taken his son's death harder than his wife realized. For weeks after Scotty's death, John had contemplated the pills behind the bathroom mirror. But then one day something changed. He just put the thought of Scotty in there with the bottles and shut the cabinet. "Every day I see my face in that mirror," he said. "I stand right there in front of it, brushing my teeth. I just no longer look at what's behind it."

The old Patricia had been unable to compartmentalize like her husband. Dr. Hartman had diagnosed her with complicated grief well before the syndrome had made it into the DSM-V, the American Psychiatric Association's handbook of disorders.

"So," Dr. Hartman said, "tell me a little about what's been happening recently."

From her purse, Patricia pulled out a cigarette and a lighter. "Oh..." she said, remembering something she had seen on the way in. "The no smoking signs outside: are those new?"

"No worries," Dr. Hartman said, pushing an ashtray over to her side of the coffee table. "Screw my fellow tenants."

She nodded and lit her cigarette, then stared at Dr. Hartman through the smoke. She didn't know where to begin, so she cut to the heart of it.

"My husband's not my husband," she said.

Dr. Hartman inhibited any facial reaction to her statement. He always strived to convey initial acceptance to anything his patients might share with him. He also excelled at remaining silent, which usually encouraged his patients to elaborate. Patricia, however, took another puff from her cigarette and waited for his response.

He said, "You'd be surprised how many people feel that way about someone they're close to. Can you go into more detail? Help me understand your specific situation?"

Patricia shrugged. "He just seems... fake. Like an actor. Even when he shows emotion, it's just to hide something."

"What do you think *he's* hiding?" Hartman asked.

"The fact that he's not my husband."

This time, the corner of Dr. Hartman's mouth twitched. Patricia spoke with such conviction she almost convinced him.

"Can you give me some examples? What specifically has made you come to this conclusion?"

Patricia flicked ashes into the tray on the coffee table. "Just last night, he asked me to put a stop to our monthly bridge games with the Schneiders. We've been playing with Mary and Joe for years, and this week was supposed to be the first time since the attack."

"What reason did John give for canceling?"

"He said it was because of his demanding schedule. But I know why he canceled. He and Joe go way back. If Joe spent any time with him..." She stubbed out her cigarette in the tray, barely smoked, and then pulled out a new one. "He would see the same things I've seen."

"Has anyone in John's immediate circle come forward with similar suspicions as yours?"

"No, he's been firing them all," Patricia said, "replacing them. Like his press liaison, Rick Walsh. Rick's been with John since the beginning. But then out of the blue, John tells him he's cutting back on his public appearances and doesn't need him anymore. So he fires Rick and immediately hires this other guy who is much younger and has far less experience."

"And have you talked to John about all of these changes?"

"He says he let Rick go because every time he saw him, he was reminded of the attack. That's the reason he gives for firing everyone."

"But you don't believe that's the true reason?"

Patricia leaned forward and pointed the unlit cigarette at the doctor. "Everyone that might have noticed John's no longer John... they've all been let go. I'm the only one who's still in his life."

Dr. Hartman grabbed his notebook from the coffee table and started to take notes. Patricia lit her second cigarette and watched him write; finally he was taking her seriously.

Still writing, Dr. Hartman said, "I need to clarify something: are you saying John has pulled back from you emotionally and verbally?"

"No, honestly he's been quite attentive. Asking me if I've slept well in the morning, if we should go out for dinner. Asking me about my day..."

"And you're interpreting this *how?*" Dr. Hartman asked. He felt confident he knew where this was going. Three years ago, when she still suffered from complicated grief, Patricia suspected her husband of having an affair. She could think of no other reason for the ice expanding between them; she had been too close to her own grief to realize it was death that had caused the cold distance. Dr. Hartman suspected John's attack in Jerusalem had triggered a similar reaction.

Patricia said, "Most of the world knows my husband as this charming, brilliant man who could bring together different people with different agendas. But behind the curtain... John was full of his own insecurities, his own misgivings about who he was and what he was capable of. The missteps that he made along the way, those all stemmed from it."

Dr. Hartman finished writing and looked up at Patricia. His assessment of John Wolfenson, based on only two sessions of couples therapy, aligned with her insights. While John was still in the womb, his father had left his mother, and so John had grown up with almost congenital abandonment issues. When he was thirteen, his mother had abandoned him too: she went for a morning jog and was struck by a car; a hit and run. He often sought comfort and guidance from others, which people generally interpreted to be charming humility, when in reality he suffered from intense self-doubt.

"Let's say, for the sake of discussion, that I agree with you about John's personal issues," Dr. Hartman said. "What point are you trying to make?"

Patricia shrugged. "The self-doubt, the agonizing over decisions, the second guessing—it's all gone. It's been replaced by this confidence, almost an *arrogance* about everything he does. It's as if the script he's reading, it's also giving him stage directions he doesn't have to question."

Dr. Hartman scribbled in his notepad again. "And when did you start feeling this way toward your husband?"

Patricia leaned forward. "You make it sound like these are just feelings that I have, that they aren't based in reality."

Hartman stopped writing and repeated his question. "When did you start feeling this way toward your husband?"

Obviously he knew the answer. Patricia said nothing and just let her cigarette fume.

The doctor set down his notebook on the coffee table and almost sighed. "Patricia, oftentimes when people go through traumatic events, they end up different... profoundly different."

"I know what you're talking about. People who come back from fighting in a war, or who lose someone to cancer."

Hartman paused to show that her words resonated with him; her son had died of leukemia.

Then he said, "It also happens when someone has been attacked by a mentally unstable woman in front of thousands of people."

Patricia pulled her purse closer and scooted to the edge of the couch cushion, poised to stand. "I knew you'd think this is like what I went through before. But it isn't. Before the attack, I was married to John Wolfenson, a man I've known for over twenty-five years—since college. There have been times when I didn't trust him. You know that better than anyone. But even then, even when I was sure he was lying to me, I never doubted that he was my husband."

"Have you had a head injury recently?" Dr. Hartman asked.

She frowned. "What kind of question is that?"

"Patricia, it's a standard question in these kinds of situations."

"No, you just don't believe me. You think I'm making this shit up."

Dr. Hartman sat forward. He wanted to show that he was engaged in her fear and anxiety, that he truly wanted to help. "I think that *you* sincerely believe everything you've told me."

"But that's different than believing me."

He glanced at her purse, at the way she was clutching it, and he decided it might not be the best time to voice his theory. Then again, waiting could make things much worse.

"Have you ever heard of Capgras syndrome?" he asked.

Patricia didn't answer him. She didn't know what the phrase meant, but because it was a medical term, it confirmed that he didn't believe her.

"Capgras syndrome," Dr. Hartman said, "is a disorder, or *delusion* that someone close to you has been replaced by an imposter."

Patricia started to cry. From the smug upturn in the corner of Dr. Hartman's lips, she knew what he thought: that he had struck at the heart of the matter. She wanted to straighten the glasses on his stupid face.

"There are several possible causes for Capgras syndrome," he said. "One of the possible causes is the result of a head injury."

Patricia wiped away her tears and stamped out her cigarette in the tray. "The last time I had a head injury is when David Banes pushed me off my damn bike when I was five. Are you saying something that happened when I was five years old is causing this?"

"No, that wouldn't be the cause," Dr. Hartman said, trying to keep his voice lower than hers to encourage a moderate tone. "So the next thing we want to rule out is some form of schizophrenia—"

She got up to leave.

"Patricia, please." He caught her by the door.

"I come in here with a real problem and immediately you're treating me like some homeless person talking to herself."

Dr. Hartman touched her arm; her whole body was tense, rearing to go. "I'm just concerned about what you're going through," he said. "I'm concerned the attack on your husband has triggered... something we need to explore."

At first he feared she would tear away from him, never come back. But then her muscles gave up and she began to sob.

Dr. Hartman gently led her to the table and handed her some Kleen-ex. "You originally came to me during one of the most difficult points in your life. Then you came again when you thought John was having an affair."

"He *was* having an affair," Patricia said as she dabbed her eyes and wiped her nose.

"I'm saying that you came to me because you trusted me," Hartman said. "And that's why you're here now, right?"

Patricia nodded. Then a thought occurred to her, and she blew her nose quickly. "Doctor, you're right. I trusted you. And so did John. He liked you. Remember he came in here for couples therapy?"

"Of course."

"So you would know if something was different with him, right?"

"I would like to think so," Dr. Hartman said.

Patricia sat down on the couch, her eyes wide and bright and red. "If I can get this guy to come in here, will you talk to him? You'll see that he's not John—he's not my husband."

Dr. Hartman nodded. "Under one condition. If I'm satisfied that he's really John, you agree to undergo a series of medical and psychological tests."

Patricia grabbed her purse. "Agreed." And then she fired up a third cigarette, which this time she smoked to the end.

CHAPTER 8

"NOT THE WHOLE CODEX GIGAS," Neal clarified on the drive from the Willard to the library in D.C. "Just the eight pages that have been missing since 1648."

"Oh, thank God," Jenna said. "I was worried you'd stolen the whole thing from the Swedes."

Despite her sarcasm, she *was* keeping a close eye on the traffic behind them. At least now she knew it wouldn't be the curators from the National Library of Sweden tailing them.

"Wait," she said, "1648? You must mean 1594."

"Well, actually..." Neal said, "no."

She mulled that over for a few minutes. Then, trying to sound offhand, she said, "So did you get these pages the same way you got Mom that stone relief for Christmas?"

"I thought we agreed to no questions."

"Oh, sorry."

"Besides, I got that relief from a dig I financed in Syria. I've told you that."

"Well, at least you didn't get it from the black market," Jenna replied, watching him from the corner of her eye. She didn't like his lack of reaction. It fit though. How else had the pages migrated to the States?

Neal parked, and they entered the library, a modern block of steel and glass. Jenna immediately hit a computer and called up the official website of the Codex Gigas.

"Make it quick," Neal said, watching over her shoulder.

"What, on this slow thing? If you wanted me to be fast, why didn't you let me use my own laptop?"

"I told you why," Neal said, refusing to repeat himself. He had forbidden her to leave a cyber-trail of the search, unless it originated from a public terminal at the library.

Jenna smiled, but made sure it looked forced. "Don't worry, I'm fairly versed. I had this friend at Brown who wrote a paper on the Codex."

Neal cocked an eyebrow. "One of your girlfriends wrote a paper and somehow you know all about it? That's quite a talent, sis."

"I proofread for *him*," Jenna replied, chastising Neal for assuming her friend was female. "I just want to brush up, check out a few photographs... if this piece of crap will ever load."

She pursed her lips and triple-clicked the mouse, although on some level she was glad for the little spinning hourglass. She needed more time to feel this whole situation out.

The first picture she opened showed a man and a woman holding up the 165-pound Codex, which stood a little over three feet tall. "Really lives up to the name Codex Gigas, doesn't it?"

Neal said nothing, and so Jenna added, "FYI, it's Latin for *giant book*."

"F my I, right."

She zoomed in on the photograph. In the white skin that dressed the wooden covers, an artist had tooled Greek key patterns, crowns, and other elaborate designs in blind. Pierced metal flourishes ornamented the corners and center of the cover. Though only the corner pieces featured griffins, they all incorporated raised circular bosses meant to lift and protect the cover from reading surfaces.

"I guess it *has* to be big," Jenna said, "considering everything it's got in it."

The book, intended to be a collection of all human knowledge, contained the entire Vulgate version of the New and Old Testaments. It also included Isidore of Seville's *Etymologiae*, Josephus's *Antiquities of the Jews*, and whole sections of medicinal cures and conjurations.

The Codex website included a scan of every single page, all 620 of them, skinned from the backs of donkeys or calves. Jenna navigated to one page in particular and waited for the browser's progress bar. "Did you know that almost everyone who's owned the Codex has been struck by some sort of misfortune?" she asked.

Neal didn't respond. Obviously he didn't want to talk about the book in public, even if they were practically whispering.

Jenna continued anyway. "The first monastery to have owned it— the Benedictine monastery at Podlažice—they found themselves in financial straits and had to pawn it. So they sold it to the White Monks in

Sedlec. I'm sure you're familiar with the ossuary there. The one with the bone chandelier."

"Yes," Neal said. He jiggled the mouse at the workstation next to her for no particular reason, then stepped back.

"Well, a lot of those bones were dumped there not long after the White Monks sold off the Codex," Jenna said. "The area got hit with the Black Death pretty hard.

"And then there's Rudolf II, the Holy Roman Emperor. During the time he had the Codex, late in the sixteenth century, he became so mental his brother ended up kicking him off the throne..."

Jenna quieted down as the page finally loaded. It showed a large illustration of the devil, framed by two tall towers. Red talons hooked from his hands and feet, and two red horns poked out of his scaly head.

The image might have been frightening if not for the ermine loincloth and lazy eyes. Jenna had always thought the illustration caricatured Satan as an idiot.

"You've heard the legend, haven't you?" Jenna asked. "About why the Codex is called the Devil's Bible?"

Neal just stood there with his hands in his pockets, so Jenna said, "Legend has it that a Benedictine monk wrote the Codex so that his monastery wouldn't wall him up alive in a cell; he'd committed some unforgivable sin or another."

"I know," Neal said. Which was obvious that he did. But Jenna's intent wasn't to inform. In fact, she hadn't used the word *actually* once.

She didn't know what her intent was, exactly, but part of her wanted to spook her brother away from whatever shady business deal he was involved in. And maybe she wanted to irritate him, so he would be more apt to let something slip.

"Anyway, the deal that the monk struck was, the monastery would spare his life if he wrote them a book containing all human knowledge, and all in a single night. Sometime around midnight, the monk realized he was screwed. So he summoned the help of the devil."

"Give me a break," her brother said. "Sounds like typical medieval superstitions."

"I hear you, Neal. But if you eliminate the legend, you're still left with a mystery. A single scribe would have taken thirty years to finish the book. *Thirty years*. A whole group of scribes could get it done quicker, and they certainly worked in groups, but then you'd see a variety of different handwriting. That's not the case. With the Codex Gigas, it's exactly the same calligraphy all the way through. That's pretty persuasive proof that only one guy was holding the quill. But if it was only one scribe, then why doesn't the text worsen with age?

"I agree the 'working with the devil in a one-night cram session' sounds like the talking point of a medieval publicist's press release, but then we wind up right back at trying to explain the perfectly uniform calligraphy throughout the book."

Neal shook his head and looked at his watch. "So did you proofread your co-ed's speech, too?" her brother asked. "Or simply write it for him?"

Whatever reaction Jenna had been going for, she wasn't getting it from Neal.

Frowning, she turned and resumed her research. After digging through the library databases, Jenna found several scholarly and less-than-scholarly sources about the missing vellum leaves. Most experts agreed that the missing pages might have described the secret monastic rules of the Benedictine order, and that the monks probably removed them in 1594 before giving the bible to Rudolf II. However, some of the less-than-scholarly sources told a different legend: that Rudolf, obsessed with the occult, had taken the pages sometime before his death because they contained supernatural rituals and spells.

Jenna printed a few pages out of the book, some samples of the handwriting and the colorful illuminated letters. She went to collect her printouts and turned back to see Neal clearing the temporary files on her library computer.

On their way to the car, Jenna said, "So am I to assume these pages are being sold off the grid?"

Neal sighed. "Look, something like the missing pages, if they were to surface legitimately, Sweden would immediately lay claim to them. Whoever was selling them would be pressured to donate the pages to the library."

"I find that laughable," Jenna said, "considering Sweden stole the Codex in the first place."

"You see, this is exactly where I don't want to go with this discussion—rights, possession, claims. This is about getting a valuable piece of history into the hands of someone who will appreciate its beauty. So what I want to know is... can you authenticate it?"

"If it's a bad forgery," she said, "yeah, no problem. But if the forger knew his business.... Even if I had a microscope, I wouldn't be one hundred percent positive."

"Well," Neal said, "that's fine because I'm looking for 'almost positive.'"

"Okay. But you need to be prepared for disappointment. There's a whole market for antiquity forgeries. It's a multimillion-dollar industry, thanks to the Internet. And the fact that these pages have suddenly re-appeared, almost on demand... sorry, the odds of a forgery are high."

"It wasn't like that," Neal said. "Apparently the pages have been on the market for a long time, but the price was too steep. Luckily, it's a price I'm willing to pay."

They arrived at his BMW, and he unlocked the car with a key fob. He opened the passenger door for his sister, but she didn't get in.

"So tell me," Jenna said. "Are you just going to flip the pages to someone else for a profit?"

"Questions, questions," Neal replied.

"I'm just saying. The book is considered one of the greatest medieval artifacts. So for you to be purchasing these pages like some sort of drug deal..."

"I know it's irresponsible."

"Actually, the word I was going for was *vulgar*."

"Come on, Jenna, don't be naïve. This kind of stuff is done all the time."

"Yeah, but not by me."

Neal's face flushed, and all the healing cuts seemed to glow pink and red. "So you won't help me?"

A taxi drove past and Neal must have seen Jenna eyeing it, because he said, "After everything I've done for you?"

Jenna crossed her arms. "I'm starting to wish I'd just taken out a few student loans here, Neal."

His face got a little redder. She had to admit, his frustration was worth it. And she did really want to get her hands on those missing pages.

"I'm going to follow through this one time," she said, "but you're going to owe *me* one. I don't ever want to be involved in something like this again, okay?"

"Understood," Neal said. He turned to walk to the driver's side, but Jenna put a hand on his shoulder.

"No, Neal, you have to promise. Promise that you'll never do something like this ever again."

He held out his little finger and said, "Pinky promise."

It was a silly thing they used to do as kids, usually after agreeing not to tattle on each other. Jenna, feeling very foolish, hooked her pinky with his.

Neal said, "Now come on. They're expecting us."

"Okay. But we need to pick up a black light on the way. And some gloves."

"What for?"

Jenna smiled. "No questions, remember?"

CHAPTER 9

THE SUN BURNT A HALO into George's eyes a second before he groaned into his pillowcase. His housekeeper, Raina, had raised his bedroom shades.

"Mr. George," she said. "¡Es mediodía!"

He had slept in his clothes from the day before, and had slept in an even older pile of laundry.

Behind a dirty sock, Raina caught sight of a framed photograph on the nightstand. In the picture, George stood with his arm around his late wife, Carri. She wore a blue blouse, which Raina now owned. Mrs. George had always been generous with her secondhand things.

Raina looked away from the picture, ignoring the burn in her eyes. She busied herself with the liquor bottles and takeout wrappers littering the floor. Some of the food scraps smelled moldy.

"What are you doing here?" George asked her. He squinted against the incoming light, which refracted along his lashes in prismatic sparkles and waves.

"Es mediodía," she said. "You need to get up and get out so I can clean."

"I thought I fired you."

"Usted es funny, Mr. George."

He *had* fired her. Because she wouldn't stop crying. When Raina first heard of the car accident, and of Carri's death, she did not come in for her afternoon cleaning. The following week, she visited the apartment but ended up weeping when she saw pictures of Carri in the entryway. George had told her to come back next week.

So she did. She managed to clean the kitchen before sobbing all over the dishwasher and clean plates; the dishware reminded her of the dinner parties she had helped Carri prepare.

"I can't have you coming in here every week and crying," George had said. "How do you think I feel?"

Raina knew exactly how he felt, but men never got that. George grieved only for his wife and himself; he couldn't see that Raina grieved for all three. Plus, he was drunk. So Raina said something mean. She would regret it later, hurting his feelings. But he had hurt hers first.

"Now I know why Mrs. George asked me never to say about the money," she said.

George took a second, but apparently he wasn't that drunk. "What're you talking about?"

Carri had given Raina money to pay for her daughter's hospital bills. Raina never understood why it was such a secret. She liked Mr. George. She thought he liked her.

"What're you talking about, Raina?"

"Nada—forget it, Mr. George."

He didn't forget it though. He slapped a couple hundred-dollar bills on the countertop and said, "I want you to leave and not come back."

So Raina stayed away for a couple of weeks and let that grumpy old Mr. George sleep in his dirty socks. He deserved it. Although deep down she knew he did not.

When Raina managed a whole day without crying—except a few tears in the shower—she showed up for her normal shift.

"Go away, Raina," George had told her. "I'm not paying you to clean anymore."

"That's all right, Mr. George. I've been stealing from you all this time. I don't need to get paid."

Every week since, she had returned to vacuum and dust. And to open George's bedroom curtains annoyingly.

"You need to get out of bed so I can lavar la ropa and sheets," she said.

George grumbled and shut his eyes to welcome the darkness. So Raina twisted one of his toes, and that got him up.

———

AFTER A HOT SHOWER, GEORGE came out of the bedroom in a fresh T-shirt and jeans. He saw Raina taking down ornaments from the Christmas tree.

"What are you doing?" he asked.

"I'm taking the tree down to la basura."

"No, don't touch it."

"But, Mr. George, it's dead." The tree slumped like an old man in need of back surgery. It had gone bald all over the unopened gifts. "Estamos febrero already."

Febrero, George thought, *February*. Time had moved so slowly he hadn't noticed it moving at all.

He took the ornament from Raina's hand and hung it back on the tree. "I said don't touch it. And leave the things underneath it alone."

Raina nodded. "Okay, Mr. George, no touch tree." She went into the bedroom to finish cleaning in there and to stifle some angry tears.

George stared at the Christmas gifts, which sparkled in the sun. One of the packages caught his eye. He picked it up, stared at it, and then decided to take it with him to the cemetery.

————

THE AFTERNOON SUN HAD DISAPPEARED behind dark clouds, and the angels and mausoleums mourned it. The smell of rain among the graves had brought with it the silence of desolation.

As George walked uphill to his wife's plot, he counted the bills in his wallet; he needed to know how long he could keep the taxi waiting at the gates. Apparently not for long. He hadn't realized how low he was on cash.

Ever since the accident, he had stopped going to work at the university where he taught evolutionary psychology. The department dean told him to take all the time he needed, assuming that George would return after Christmas break. But after the first week of winter semester when George still didn't show up for work, the dean started to leave encouraging voicemails, which went unanswered.

His last message had been more pointed than encouraging: "Hey, George. Once again, just reaching out to you. We're sort of at a cross-roads with your classes. The substitute absolutely hates it, and some of the students are dropping out for the full refund." He sighed, or pretended to. "I know this must be a difficult time for you. But I also believe Carri would want you to get back to what you do best. Give me a call."

George had deleted the message almost instantly after playback. How dare anyone presume what Carri would want? The reality was she criticized his field of expertise, and believed that people often used evolutionary psychology to justify bad behavior. Like that time George got mad at her one night for chatting up a handsome bartender. "George Wyatt," she'd said, smiling, but angry that he didn't trust her, "are you jealous?"

"You're damn right I am, and I'm not apologizing. Male jealousy is a genetic trait caused by thousands of years of selective pressure. Way before chastity belts or paternity tests—there were only two surefire ways to keep the male competition out of your woman's genes. One, guard her with extreme prejudice. Or two, eliminate the previously aforementioned male competition."

He ended up rethinking his thesis while sleeping on the living room couch.

At the top of Lullaby Hills, George stooped, out of breath. His wife's misspelled headstone had been replaced with a temporary marker, correctly spelled.

"Merry Christmas," he said to the grave marker as he worked the gift out of his pocket. "I know you don't like technology, but..." He opened it and held it up. "I got you a digital camera."

Carri had been the last person on earth who still used film; at least that's what George had told her. "You're like a neo-luddite," he'd once said. "In fact, I think you download all those viruses to my computer on purpose."

She had laughed.

George powered on the camera and turned the digital viewfinder toward the grave marker. "Here's the best part," he said. "Pictures. Just some things and places out of our everyday lives. I wanted to prove to you how easy it was."

He cycled through a few of them.

"Look at this one, Carri, your lifeline throughout the day: the coffeemaker. And here's our unmade bed. And your... car."

He quickly navigated to the next picture. This one he had taken from their bedroom balcony, looking down at Carri one day as she walked home from the gym. She wore the same Washington Redskins cap she always wore, including the day she died.

Drops splashed and beaded on the camera's digital screen. At first he mistook tears for rain.

He clicked forward again and found a closer shot of Carri walking toward their apartment. She was smiling for no apparent reason. Oddly, George had forgotten that about her, how she always smiled.

It reminded him of something she once said about photographs: "I love them because they capture a moment that would otherwise be lost; they allow that moment to live on forever."

George dried the screen with his sleeve. He had ignored it until now—it had been too painful to pursue—but Carri had been trying to tell him something. Her pictures weren't the only place she lived on, and finally he understood what he had to do.

CHAPTER 10

ETAN COULD HEAR FOOTSTEPS. He tried to stop breathing, but could only hold his breath a few short seconds before gasping for air. He was about to try again, but the closet door slid open.

"There you are. Everyone is searching for you."

Etan looked up as Mr. Marcus loomed over him. The bearded man looked as intimidating as the first time they met years ago.

"Etan, is that blood?!"

Mr. Marcus knelt down to the boy's curled up body. In the darkness of the closet he probably had not noticed that Etan was bleeding from his stomach.

"I'm sorry, sir... Sorry about everything."

He wanted to cry, but he beat back the urge. Etan knew Mr. Marcus would already be ashamed of what he had done. Tears would only add to the shame.

"Okay, here's what we're going to do. I'm going to lift you up and get you on this bed. Sound like a plan?"

He did not wait for Etan to respond. Mr. Marcus scooped him up and carried him to the bed, where he laid the boy down.

After the pain subsided a bit, Etan reached for the rooster claw around his chest.

"Yes, it's still there, Etan, perfectly intact. No need to worry," Mr. Marcus said. "Now, I need you to lie still while I call someone who can help."

A phone sat on the nightstand nearby. Mr. Marcus picked it up and dialed a number. Waiting for the connection, he looked at Etan, and their eyes connected.

"What is your name?" asked Mr. Marcus.

"Orisas"

"That's right. Never forget who you have become."

Etan nodded.

"And what are we all trying to achieve?"

"Olódùmarè."

This time Mr. Marcus didn't react to his answer. Etan could see the disappointment in his eyes. For years Mr. Marcus had worked with him. Now in one single night, Etan's actions had ruined everything.

He started feeling lightheaded.

"I need your help..." Mr. Marcus said to someone on the phone.

Then everything went black.

———

"ARE YOU ALL RIGHT?"

Etan opened his eyes.

"Sir?"

Everyone in the coach section of the plane was staring at him.

"You must have been dreaming, sir."

Etan nodded and touched the flight attendant on the arm. "Thank you so much. I'm sorry if I disturbed anyone."

"No worries, sir. You let me know if you need anything else." She smiled and moved up the aisle.

Etan took a deep breath, then looked out the window. He waited a few seconds, then began scanning the cabin to see if the other passengers were still looking at him. Everyone seemed to be absorbed in some new gadget or another. He let out a sigh of relief.

The redeye flight from Nice Côte d'Azur Airport to Washington, D.C. would put him in the United States in the morning. He was excited to be following up so swiftly on the lead provided by his travel agent. But he hated falling asleep with anyone around him.

———

A MAN LIKE CARLO VENOVA would say anything to avoid having his skull added to Etan's collection. Yet Etan believed the travel agent's admission that Ambassador Tottone possessed the Black Pages.

At 350,000 square feet, and with a park surrounding it, the French embassy resembled a modern-day fortress. Getting past the security cameras and armed guards would require a team of trained operatives. So Etan created a plan that would accommodate and even play to the strength of his status as a lone operative. He would strike tomorrow, early in the morning, when all the vehicles piled up at the front gate for a security check. As Ambassador Tottone waited in the long line, his diplomatic standing, international-jet-setting lifestyle, and access to the wealthy and powerful would be leveled to an unemployed loser standing in line for his welfare check. A single operative on foot could swiftly gain entrance to the vehicle, kill both the driver and the ambassador with an automatic pistol, snatch the Black Pages, and be out before embassy security even started to register the honking horns and panicked drivers in the other Town Cars.

With a plan chalked out, all that was left was the transfusion before his operation. Cold water for blood. Etan visualized the process. Cold water for blood. Then he spoke the words.

Cold water for blood in the face of danger.

He whispered it to himself several times, made it his mantra. The most cherished of his cherished rules of engagement.

While he continued to observe the comings and goings of the embassy from the vantage of a park bench, his phone rumbled with a text message from his employer; the address of the hotel where Tottone usually stayed while in the States.

Etan was disappointed. He had been constructing his plan for the last several hours, and now he probably had to scrap it. He drove immediately to Georgetown, but all along the way, he hoped the French diplomat had changed residences to some unknown location, which would force Etan to have his fun at the embassy.

Less than an hour later, he cruised past the John Jay Royal Hotel. It was a far cry from a fortress. More like an unguarded glass palace. If the French ambassador was indeed staying there, then obtaining the Black Pages had become *fait accompli.*

———

ETAN STAKED OUT THE FRONT ENTRANCE of the hotel from a nearby café, where a college kid was finger-picking a guitar on a tiny stage. He rubbed his right eye, feeling some irritant behind the brown lens, but resisted the urge to retreat to the restroom.

After a couple of hours, a Lincoln Town Car pulled up to the hotel's valet. The driver, doubling as a bodyguard, opened the back door for a thin man in a thinly tailored suit, French Ambassador Arnaud Tottone.

The diplomat's arrival, so early in the day, surprised Etan. He notified his employer that he had eyeballed the French ambassador at the John Jay Hotel. Then he set his phone on his lap and waited for a response. His employer, in situations like this, never allowed more than a few minutes to go by without responding. But, even as he waited, Etan tried to anticipate what his directive would be and began to strategize about the best way to acquire the number of the diplomat's hotel room.

He was still waiting for a response from his employer when the diplomat reappeared with his driver. The guard ushered Tottone into the waiting vehicle like the ambassador was an expectant mother. Except Tottone wasn't bearing a potential child—he was carrying a large leather portfolio.

Damn it! Etan thought, rushing to pay his bill. Two plans up in smoke. Tottone was moving the pages at that exact moment.

In his rental car, Etan used all of his driving skills to catch up as the diplomat's driver entered traffic toward the Capital Beltway. After achieving visual contact with his target, it was hard for him to slip back to a four- or five-car distance, but he did so nonetheless. That's why Etan never considered himself anything less than a professional.

After following the Town Car for over thirty minutes, he received a message from his employer.

Acquire the merchandise at all cost. Wet removal. Any collateral stain is acceptable. Leave no residue.

Etan erased the message. He didn't need a reminder.

———

NEAL GOT LESS AND LESS TALKATIVE as he and Jenna approached their rendezvous near Manassas, Virginia. He kept his eyes fixed straight ahead as he sped down I-66, so Jenna took the opportunity to concentrate on her printouts from the library. She jumped when he broke the silence.

"Hard to believe, but that's where Bull Run was fought." He pointed to the acreage beside the freeway, a mix of woodlands, meadows, and streams. Bull Run was the first major land battle in the Civil War, and Jenna knew quite a bit about it.

"Well, actually..." she said, planning to explain that Bull Run was a Northern reference to the battle, and that the Southern reference, the one generally accepted by historians, was First Manassas. But Neal gave her a look, and she smiled like a smartass... and then they both started laughing.

"Hey," Neal said as they both settled down, "you remember when Dad did that Civil War re-enactment at Fredericksburg? We all had a picnic and then watched him get it on with the rebels?"

Jenna shook her head. "No, I was, like, four when Dad left, Neal. All I really remember are those postcards he used to send after he left. You know, the ones from Cambodia, Columbia or wherever he was that

92

month? And he'd write those generic motivational slogans on the back?"

"Oh yeah, like, 'Stay in school!'"

"Or, 'Take care of your mother!'"

"Or, 'Never give up on your dreams!'"

Jenna smiled. "Long-distance parenting sucks."

"Yeah, it's no wonder Mom told him to stop sending those stupid things. What'd she call him? A gypsy with a fistful of postcards?"

"She called him a lot worse than that."

"He wasn't that bad," Neal said, but Jenna had never known her father. And so she had a side to herself she didn't know either. An angle to her face, an unfamiliar expression. She recognized this stranger in Neal as well, a part of him that hadn't come from their mother. Jenna wondered if he was showing more of that side today.

They exited the freeway and drove for a few minutes into the cold pastoral silence of the countryside.

———

ETAN HAD NEVER TRAVELLED this far south of the capital, and he found the scenery both picturesque and tacky; large meadows gave way to strip malls and tourist traps. He followed the Town Car past Manassas to a cheap motel off the highway, isolated perfectly in the shade.

Etan hid his rental in the weeds across the street, in a used car lot abandoned by everything but the trash.

He peered stealthily over his dashboard as Tottone's Town Car parked at the motel.

The driver wore a suit jacket and a weapon underneath. He scanned the lot for anything suspicious. Then he escorted Tottone inside. Under his arm, the diplomat carried the leather portfolio.

The Black Pages, Etan thought. After two years of preparing and tracking the artifact through the black market, now only the distance of a parking lot and two men stood in his way.

His job had gotten easier and easier, from fortress to hotel to motel. However, all the changes in his plan hadn't allowed time to devise a disguise. If he pursued the two men into the motel, he ran the risk of cameras. On the other hand, if he stayed in his car and Tottone sold the pages, Etan risked losing track of the relic.

He knew of only one disguise. Inside a tiny saline capsule, he tucked away his brown contact lens. Birth certificates did not document eye color. And Etan's driver's license claimed that he had two green eyes; his alias Paul Seeger had two brown. Hopefully tonight, one green eye would be the only thing witnesses could remember.

He got out of his car and started across the street. He told himself that the motel was old and in disrepair and probably didn't have video surveillance in the lobby or halls.

Just as Etan opened the glass door to the lobby, a middle-aged man wearing extra-extra-extra-large sweat pants and an equally large T-shirt clogged the entrance. Etan couldn't shoulder past the man, so he had no other choice but to step aside and watch through the glass as the diplomat and his driver entered one of two motel elevators.

Patience, Etan thought as he waited for the tourist to get the hell out of his way. The man's trolley luggage caught on the doorframe, and he spent several seconds yanking it loose. He finally made it out, and Etan smiled at him. The tourist didn't return the courtesy and left his body odor lingering in the doorway.

My God, Etan thought, passing through the stink. Just a few years ago, the people in this country had been fat and happy, but now in this economy they were simply fat.

At the check-in counter of the lobby, an elderly black woman occupied the motel employee. The thermometer in the woman's room wasn't working, so the employee was doing everything to appease her. Neither of them noticed Etan. He kept his head down in case of any cameras in the lobby.

Tottone's elevator was on its way back down, but from which floor Etan couldn't be sure. The indicator seemed to have just lit up the number three, so he guessed and took the stairs.

On the fourth-floor landing, he peered through a small window in the stairwell door. No one occupied the hallway. And, again, he saw no cameras.

Etan entered the hallway, head still down just in case. He stood silent, listening, then proceeded casually, pausing at each door to eavesdrop.

Through one of the doors, he heard a television and wondered whether Tottone had turned it up to conceal the transaction. *Maybe*, he thought, but decided to keep moving.

At room 418, he heard voices. He pressed his ear to the wood and distinctly heard a French accent.

Tottone.

Etan retreated to the stairwell and watched from behind the small window.

CHAPTER 11

J ENNA ALMOST COULDN'T BELIEVE IT when they pulled into the parking lot of the Real Comfort Motel.

"This is it?" she asked, appraising the four-story brick structure and its annexed breakfast diner. It needed a fresh coat of paint and a thorough roach bomb. "This is where we're going to examine a document that could be worth millions of dollars?"

Neal shut off the car. "What'd you expect, the lobby of the Four Seasons? Come on—we're late." He got out of the car.

Jenna gathered her library pages and the plastic bag full of her recently purchased items: a black light, a magnifying glass, and a pair of surgeon's gloves. She glanced out through the windshield to make sure Neal wasn't leaving her behind. He stood just in front of the car, scoping out the area.

Police posed the greatest threat, Jenna figured. Recently while digging up an artifact for a game of Spot the Fake, she had read a report by the Supreme Council of Antiquities estimating that, in the last five years, officials had recovered over five thousand stolen or smuggled artifacts in Egypt alone.

But if cops posed a problem this far off the grid, so did crooks. Neal and his associates would never report a robbery, which made them perfect prey for criminals.

Neal's gaze paused on a Lincoln Town Car parked in the back of the lot, close to the main road. Jenna noticed the vehicle's odd license plate, its light-blue background and curved red header.

The Virginia DMV offered a variety of special plates, everything from Veterans of Foreign Wars to Ducks Unlimited. So Jenna assumed the Lincoln's plates showcased some special interest. But then in the header she spotted the word *DIPLOMAT* and the seal of the Department of State: a bald eagle looking toward the olive branch of peace, ignoring the arrows of war.

A diplomat? Jenna thought. *At a roach motel?*

Supposedly, the second and third letters in the plate's number represented the diplomat's country, but *DJ* didn't ring any bells.

Neal glanced back at Jenna, who quickly ignored the Town Car. Her brother tapped his watch. Jenna nodded, took a deep breath, and stepped outside.

Despite her long legs, she had trouble pacing her brother into the motel. He bypassed the front desk and cut straight to the elevator. Jenna caught up as the doors opened and Neal stepped into the car.

On the ride upstairs, she tried to think of something to say. Maybe something funny to test how nervous he was. She couldn't think of anything fast enough.

The elevator opened onto the fourth floor, and Neal turned left with no hesitation.

He's been here before, Jenna thought, *damn*. She had hoped this was her brother's first foray into the black market.

Neal stopped at room 418 and knocked on the door.

"Who is it?" said a voice from the other side.

"It's me," Neal replied.

Jenna heard a chain disengaging

———

THROUGH THE SMALL GLASS WINDOW of the stairwell door, Etan watched a man and a woman emerge from the elevator. Even before the couple entered room 418, he knew they were the buyers.

The woman was younger, perhaps in her late twenties and casually dressed; her hair looked as if she had rolled out of the wrong side of the bed and missed the shower.

The man, at least a few years older, dressed so well his shirt probably sported his initials monogrammed on the cuffs. Someone of his class did not belong in a Virginian motel that probably still had vibrating beds you could turn on for a quarter.

As Etan descended the staircase, he calculated his reaction to all possible outcomes of the situation. Everything led him to the same conclusion: follow the leather portfolio.

He and his employer were interested only in the pages... and anyone who came in contact with them.

Wet Removal.

If a deal didn't go down, Etan would get the license plate of the buyer and track them.

Any collateral is acceptable.

He already knew how to track Tottone, so Etan could circle back at another time to eliminate him and his bodyguard.

No residue.

Etan entered the lobby, which was empty except for the check-in employee, busy on the phone, yelling at the thermostat repairman.

Etan hadn't seen any cameras when he entered, but as before, he played it safe. As he approached the exit, Etan lowered his head as if to count all the stains on the carpet.

———

JENNA AND NEAL WERE GREETED at the door by an attractive woman in her thirties. If the Codex pages were half as fake as this blonde's dye job, Jenna would have no problem exposing the artifact.

"Sorry we're late," Neal said. "We hit some traffic along the way."

The blonde nodded and waved them in. Her vanilla perfume mixed with stale cigarette smoke, which over the years had permeated the very walls and fabrics of the room.

On the other side of the bed, near a window with drawn curtains, two men flanked a large leather portfolio, the kind in which art students carried their work. It sat on the carpet between their leather shoes.

That's it, Jenna thought, *the pages.* She couldn't help but feel a little flutter in her stomach.

The older man, somewhere in his fifties, wore a suit tailored so perfectly to his thin frame that it had become a part of him. He kept his beard neatly trimmed.

The younger man beside him had dressed casually, yet he looked anything but relaxed. His eyes flicked from the plastic bag in Jenna's hands to the cuts on Neal's face. He adjusted the hang of his suit jacket, to better conceal the bulge beneath it, perhaps.

As Ms. Vanilla shut the door and reengaged the chain, Jenna thought about asking her very nicely to let her the hell out.

But then Neal crossed the room and shook hands with the bearded man, and Jenna knew it was too late to retreat.

"Great to meet you," Neal said.

The bearded man nodded. "Pleasure. We just got here ourselves."

He's French, Jenna thought, noting the accent. She immediately flashed on the license plate of the Town Car she had seen in the parking lot.

"Shall we get started?" Neal asked.

"Yes, yes, that will be good. I've got a plane to catch." The Frenchman set the leather portfolio on the bed and pulled out a thin stack of vellum leaves, each encased in a clear plastic envelope. Moving slowly, carefully, he spread all four leaves, a total of eight pages, into a grid on the coverlet. Then he stepped back and fixed his eyes on Jenna, who stood there with her mouth agape.

Neal nudged her, and she almost dropped her references. "You're up," he said.

Everyone was staring at her: the blonde, her brother, the young man with the bulge beneath his jacket.

Jenna nodded and took a step toward the bed. The floor beneath her seemed to tilt, and the heady mix of men's cologne, age-old smoke, and vanilla almost made her sick.

Just focus on the pages, she told herself. She had always dreamt of something like this, a lost relic, missing from the pages of time. But in her dream she always imagined she would be kneeling in a dark, dank cave, not in a dark, dank motel room, wanting to hold her nose.

Jenna set down her things and quickly skimmed each page.

The library printer only produced black-and-white copies, so Jenna wouldn't be able to match the color of the vellum and the vibrant illuminations of the text. She tried her best to remember the color of the images online, and she thought the pages arranged on the bed before her matched well. Even the style of calligraphy appeared to be very similar. Superficial observations, to be sure—any forger worth his weight in quills could get past the first smell test—but encouraging factors nonetheless.

"Can we get some more light in here?" Jenna asked Neal.

"The curtains stay closed," the Frenchman said.

Jenna looked to her brother, and in the corner of her eye, the guy with the bulge under his jacket tensed up.

"That's not what I meant. Sunlight is actually bad for vellum," Jenna said. "What I need is more lamplight."

The blonde moved to one of the nightstands and clicked on the lamp, then moved it closer to the bed. "We're lucky," she said. "Most of these motels have gone green and use these low-wattage bulbs. It's like reading in a cave."

Jenna forced a smile, acknowledging the woman's attempt to get everybody to relax. Although it didn't seem to work on Mr. Business Casual with the obviously concealed gun. She looked over at her brother, who nodded for her to begin.

So Jenna took a deep breath and then started to authenticate the eight pages under the energy-inefficient light.

CHAPTER 12

As SOON AS THE TAXI PULLED UP to the main entrance of Broad Run Hospital, George began to tremble and sweat. The last time he had been here, he had come in an ambulance, and had left without his wife.

George almost told the taxi driver just to drive him back to the train station, but he ended up paying his fare instead and got out of the vehicle. The taxi left him standing in the shadow of the facility.

Inside, at the glass enclosure around the reception desk, a dozen people stood in line. George waited about twenty minutes before it was his turn to speak to one of the nurses. He asked for Dr. Tellen, the ER surgeon who had worked on his wife the day she was brought in.

"I'll page him, but it could be awhile for him to respond to a non-emergency situation," the nurse said.

"That's all right. I have all the time in the world."

George sat in the waiting room. For the briefest moment, the past and present overlaid, so that he was waiting outside the ER again, equally dreading and hoping for news about his wife. Dr. Tellen had operated on her for over two hours, at first to stop the bleeding from her head, then to address her internal injuries.

After more than an hour since the nurse had paged Dr. Tellen, George stood up to leave. But then Dr. Tellen emerged from behind the receptionist enclosure, and George greeted him instead.

"Mr. Wyatt, how are you doing?" the doctor said.

"Not very good. But thanks for taking the time to see me."

"Of course. What can I do for you?"

"I remember that when my wife... after she died and you, um..."

"Harvested her heart."

"Yes," George said, frowning. The word *harvested* sounded emotionless. You harvested carrots, not organs. "You offered to give me the name of the recipient of my wife's heart," George said. "I didn't want it at the time, but now..."

"Now, you would like to have the name?"

George nodded.

Dr. Tellen nodded too. "I understand. Wait here a minute." He disappeared behind the receptionist enclosure, into a back room.

George almost sat down again, but his legs felt restless. He paced back and forth for about ten minutes until the doctor returned with a folded business card.

"The recipient's information is on the back," Dr. Tellen said, handing George the card. "He lives in New York City. At least he did when he received your wife's organ. If you need more information, just call the business number on the card. It's for the organ donation headquarters in Richmond that handled your wife's case."

"Thanks," George said. He stashed the folded card in his breast pocket. Then he said goodbye and hoped to never see the doctor again.

CHAPTER 13

"I NEED TO TAKE THE PAGES out of these sleeves," Jenna told the Frenchman. "I need to determine the age of the vellum, if that's okay."

Neal looked over at the Frenchman, who shrugged.

"Remember, I have a flight," he said.

"How long do I have?"

"An hour."

Jenna shot a look at her brother, who had mentioned nothing about a time limit. "That's not going to work."

"Jenna..." Neal said

"No, I need more time. I've got to do an age test, an ink test, a style examination—not to mention a translation. Can't you just reschedule your flight?"

"No," the Frenchman said, though he seemed like the kind of guy who made his own schedule. "We have until that alarm goes off." He pointed to the bedside clock and instructed the blonde to set it.

"Fine," Jenna said. She didn't want to argue. She had too much work to do.

Jenna put on her new surgical gloves, then carefully pulled out each vellum leaf and set it on its plastic sleeve. Under normal circumstances she would have conducted a radiocarbon test to measure the carbon-14 in the material. But since crappy little motel rooms didn't come with amenities such as spectrometers, she had to work with the tools she had.

Besides, a carbon test would have only dated the death of the animal from which the vellum had been skinned; it would not have told her when the scribe had inked it.

"This is definitely donkey or calfskin," she said, taking in the texture and smell and grain of the vellum. "The original Codex came from the same kind of animal. And the discoloration, the wear and tear... See how this part looks nice and cured, and this part looks chafed? I'd say it's consistent with fifteenth century stock, at least."

"Excellent," said the Frenchman.

"Actually," Jenna said, "it could just mean that a forger recycled old vellum. He could have scraped off any existing text and then simply wrote his own... Although I should be able to tell if that's the case."

From her plastic bag, she retrieved the magnifying glass and inspected the eight pages.

"It hasn't been scraped, I assure you," said the Frenchman.

Jenna didn't take his word for it, but gave him credit for accuracy. "Mmm, yeah, looks like you're right."

She took out the black light, which she plugged in near the bed. "Mind if I shut off the lights?"

The Frenchman agreed, so the blonde clicked off the bedside lamps; Neal caught the wall switch.

Fortunately, clouds had dampened the sunlight, and a thick, dark material composed the curtains; only a dull glow bled through.

Jenna turned on the black light and held it over one of the leaves.

"What are you looking for?" the blonde asked.

"I want to see how the ink reacts." Jenna moved to the next leaf to see if it, too, exhibited the same qualities. "There are two types of medieval inks. One is made out of metal, which tends to fluoresce in UV light. The other is made of crushed insect nests—"

"Yuck," said the blonde.

Jenna nodded and leaned closer to the page. "The insect ink doesn't radiate a great deal, and it's used throughout the Codex Gigas. That's a major clue the book might've been written by a single hand: the ink type never changes."

"So obviously insect ink was used here," the Frenchman said.

"Well..." Jenna quickly scanned the remaining pages, unwilling to make the same assumption but confident of the results. "This ink is brown and lackluster. So it's certainly not a metal ink. And I'd say the color and quality is consistent with insect nests, so, yeah, you're probably right."

"Good," Neal said. "So what do you think?"

Jenna clicked the bedside lamp on again. "I think I need to do a whole lot more tests."

The Frenchman sighed and looked at his watch, and the bodyguard next to him adjusted the holster hidden underneath his suit jacket.

Neal said, "Of course. Do what you need."

Smart man, Jenna thought, admiring her brother's resilience to the pressure tactics. He didn't care about the Frenchman's flight, and neither did she. The one thing she and her brother had in common at the moment was ancient history.

"The ruling on these pages is promising," she said, hoping to brighten the room a little.

"Ruling?" the blonde asked.

"Yeah, it's like the lines on a piece of college-ruled paper." Jenna indicated the 106 horizontal lines down the length of the page, and then the six vertical ones framing the two columns. "In the Codex, the lines were pressed into the vellum with a tool called a point. That's why there's a furrow on one side and a ridge on the other. It's also what's so encouraging about these pages.

"First of all, in the early thirteenth century, ruling by point rather than by plummet or crayon was conservative. And it was always done on hair sides, so that the versos and rectos—"

"The *what?*"

"The left and right pages," Jenna explained. "In the typical manuscript, ridged versos face ridged rectos, and furrows face furrows. The Codex is kind of... the black sheep. Its ruling is consistently done on the rectos. That means ridges and furrows face each other, just like on these pages here."

"Wow," the blonde said, surprising Jenna with her genuine interest. "So what are the holes for?" She pointed to the pinpricks along the four margins of each leaf.

Jenna said, "You know how when you're drawing a straight line, sometimes you'll make a dot at both ends first? And then you'll use those dots to line up the ruler?"

"Yeah."

"Well these little pinpricks along the margins are like those little dots. They help the scribe draw straight ruling. Also—" Jenna said, but the Frenchman cut her off.

"Enough of the lesson."

"Fine," Jenna said, and turned back to the pages. *Sheesh!* Even with an English accent, he would have sounded rude.

Okay, smell test over, she thought. It was time to analyze the handwriting and content.

The scribe of the Codex Gigas used a distinct twelve-point calligraphy, possibly self-taught. A decent forger could imitate it, but not without a "forger's tremor." Original handwriting comes in quick, smooth motions, but forgeries stutter and stop in blunt ends and broken lines. Jenna used both her UV light and then her magnifying glass to scrutinize all eight pages. Her meticulous examination revealed no sign of a hesitant or nervous hand.

Next, she scanned the content for flaws in period detail. As most experts suspected, the first four pages listed monastic rules for the Benedictine order: everything from proper behavior of a monk sent on a journey, to the monastic goal of avoiding the outside world.

On the fifth, sixth and seventh pages, however, Jenna found something unexpected.

"Quatrains," she said.

The Frenchman looked confused. "What?"

"Quatrains. A stanza of poetry consisting of four lines. Like the predictions Nostradamus used to write."

"I know what a quatrain is," the Frenchman said. "There are some in the pages?"

"In three of the eight, yeah. Twelve stanzas in all." Jenna translated the first quatrain from Latin:

It was upon the fall when the light
From the morning star came upon me
We were thusly joined in isolation
A labor of redemption and rebellion

She had barely read the last word when her brother said, "Jenna, you're here to authenticate, not translate." For the first time since they arrived, he looked agitated.

"Neal, I need to translate so I can authenticate. Any malapropism or historically inaccurate phrase would be indication of a forgery."

He closed his eyes and nodded, but his agreement was cursory. Neal was clearly frustrated.

Jenna put the observation out of mind and translated the rest of the quatrains.

After several minutes, the Frenchman broke the silence. "Why don't you read them all aloud?"

"I thought you had a plane to catch," said Neal.

"I'm suddenly curious. Aren't you?"

Neal shook his head. "No, not really."

The Frenchman turned to Jenna. "Okay, then at least translate the final quatrain."

Jenna looked over at her brother, who barely nodded.

In her head she went through the quatrain one more time before speaking the English translation aloud. "This is the testament of our joined wills / A sunrise that blinds, nay a dark horizon which fades / One that awaits the deceived / It will be a sunrise that blinds us all."

The Frenchman's expression was blank and hard to read. "What does it mean?"

"I don't know," Jenna said. "I'm just giving you the translation, not the interpretation."

The Frenchman looked puzzled. "Are you surprised pages from the Codex Gigas would have quatrains?"

The Frenchman's question was reassuring. Someone who was knowingly trafficking in a forgery would never make such an inquiry. He would have no motivation to even raise the issue.

"Not necessarily," Jenna answered. "The use of quatrains was very popular during the period of time this text was allegedly written."

"Speaking of *authentic*," Neal said, tapping his watch, "can we finish authenticating the document?"

Jenna responded by turning her attention to the eighth and final page. She was excited to take another look at it because, on her initial UV scan and magnification, she noticed the text here had been written in modified medieval Latin... interspersed with a strange code.

Jenna studied the first paragraph:

Obsecro te Aieqanƶ bX✳X⅄
statim abire ex hoc lunchkal ⅄X2Ƽ9H
quem ⅄X2Ƽ9H omnipotens fecit suo ⅄✳Ƽ⅄9

While examining the rest of the text on the page, Jenna began to recognize a few symbols used in the strange encryption. The characters both intrigued her... and troubled her.

"Can I use the restroom really quick?"

"What for?" Neal said.

Jenna rolled her eyes. "What do you think?"

The Frenchman said, "If you're in there when the alarm goes off, the pages leave with me."

Jenna checked the clock. She hadn't realized it, but her examination had burned up fifty-six minutes. "I'll just be a second," she said.

She shut and locked the thin bathroom door, then shut the toilet lid and sat on it. She took out her smartphone and began to text Raymond. Neal would have killed her if he knew. But what her brother didn't know wouldn't kill him. The same applied to Raymond.

Quick game of Spot the Fake, Jenna typed, trying for playfulness instead of conspicuousness. *Eight lost pages from the Codex Gigas, encoded with words from Hildegard of Bingen's Lingua Ignota: possibly authentic or automatic fake? Why?*

She waited, stared at the door. She wondered what time it was in London. Would Raymond be at work, or in bed? He used his phone as an alarm clock, so he would hear her incoming text. He usually would wake up and answer if he heard her ringtone.

"Two minutes," the Frenchman called.

She flushed the toilet and then washed her hands to buy some time. The bathroom mirror made her hair look worse than it was. With her luck, she'd have the same bad hair when the police took her mugshot.

The alarm in the other room began to buzz.

Damn it, Raymond.

Jenna returned to the main room, drying her hands on her pants—which suddenly beeped. Her phone was signaling an incoming text.

Everyone looked at her. Neal frowned at her pocket.

Jenna tried to play it down. "I guess I have no other choice but to announce that I'm done with the examination," she said.

"Yeah? So what do you think?" Neal asked, thankfully losing interest in the curious noise from her phone.

She looked over at the Frenchman and his bodyguard, then glanced at the blonde. To Neal she said, "You want to talk about it here?"

"Absolutely. If the pages aren't authentic, they need to hear why."

"Well, I believe they're genuine," Jenna said, praying that Raymond hadn't just texted her evidence to the contrary.

"How sure are you about their authenticity?" Neal asked.

"Like I told you: without a carbon test or a microscope, I can't be one hundred percent positive. There's some content in there I wouldn't have expected, but it's still consistent with the artifact's time period. So allowing for the limited tests I was able to perform, and the time limitations imposed, I'm willing to declare that I believe these are the missing pages from the Codex Gigas."

Without another word, Neal pulled out his smartphone and started punching in some numbers while the Frenchman and bodyguard watched.

Almost as a complete afterthought, he turned to Jenna and offered her the keys to his car. "Can you wait out in the Beemer, sis? We'll only be a few minutes."

Before Jenna could answer, the blonde disengaged the security chain. Jenna took her brother's keys and said goodbye, but no one replied. The blonde just nodded and half smiled as Jenna made her way into the hall.

Then the door shut behind her, and she could hear the chain reengage.

CHAPTER 14

B ACK IN THE ABANDONED CAR LOT, Etan waited in his rental, stroking the rooster's claw that hung around his neck. Fear of failure preyed heavily upon him. He needed to cover this scenario from too many angles.

Suddenly, he was in play.

The woman with the mussed hair emerged from the motel. Her well-dressed partner was not with her, nor was she carrying the leather portfolio. Etan was genuinely surprised and disappointed. He felt certain they were the buyers.

The young woman was reading a text on her phone as she approached a BMW, one of two expensive cars in the lot. Etan, who had excellent instincts for these things, had already copied the Beemer's license plate number into his pocket notebook, right beside Tottone's.

He tapped his fingers on the steering wheel. What if the French diplomat emerged with the leather portfolio? What would he do about the woman and her well-dressed accomplice? He would have to assume they saw the Black Pages, and would have to wipe up the residue, as per his instructions.

Etan decided to just wait and see who exited the motel next, hoping fate would spare him from a difficult choice.

———

ON HER WAY ACROSS THE PARKING LOT, Jenna read Raymond's text in between glancing over her shoulder.

Possibly authentic, he had said. *The Codex was written close to a century after Hildegard's code, but both were part of the same Benedictine Order, written just miles apart.*

Which would make the degrees of separation close, even without Kevin Bacon as a go-between, he wrote a second later, unable to resist a joke. *Sneaky and cheeky bunch of do-gooders if you're also asking me.*

Thank God, Jenna thought. The pages she had just authenticated could be, in fact, authentic. Which she hadn't doubted until encountering the code on the eighth page.

Now that she thought about it, though, the code corroborated the legend of Emperor Rudolf II removing the pages for his cabinet of curiosities; Hildegard's arcane symbols would have intrigued such a man obsessed with unraveling the mysteries of the universe.

Jenna let herself into Neal's BMW. The smell of cushy leather seats and spearmint comforted her, but barely; memories of her brother were no longer as calming.

She glanced up at the motel's fourth-story windows. Obviously, Neal had dismissed her because he planned to complete the transaction. Jenna had already called the whole thing vulgar, so he clearly wanted to spare her from witnessing the grease of the deal.

She already knew he hadn't carried the money with him to close the transaction; that much cash would have bulged worse than a gun beneath a suit jacket. No, Neal's smartphone was his billfold; his currency was ordinary routing numbers sent over a banking network.

Jenna remembered something, and she tilted the rearview mirror to reflect the Town Car with the diplomatic plates.

Quick trivia, she texted Raymond, her brain outpacing her thumbs. *What country does DJ mean on a diplomat's plate?*

After a minute or two, Raymond said, *France. Now leave me alone.* He punctuated the text with a smiley face.

Sorry, Jenna said, sincerely. But she had to bug him one more time. *I just saw a French diplomat. He seemed pretty important. Wish I knew his name. Bye!*

Could be the French ambassador, Raymond shot back. *Arnaud Tottone. Did you get a pic? Where'd you see him?*

Jenna shut her cell, now really sorry to have piqued his interest. Any more questions would have led to unfortunate answers, because Jenna didn't believe she could lie.

So, the fancy car parked at this seedy little motel belonged to the French ambassador to America. Made sense. The biggest hurdle for black market items was customs, which a foreign diplomat could easily sidestep.

So then who's the blonde? Jenna wondered. *Neal's contact to the black market?* She assumed her brother not only knew the woman, he knew her well. When they had first entered the motel room, Neal had quickly introduced himself to Tottone and his bodyguard, but had completely ignored the blonde. Familiars did that sometimes.

From the main door to the motel, Neal exited. Luckily he was too busy taking a phone call to notice Jenna readjusting the BMW's rearview mirror.

Neal was alone, aside from the voice in his ear. Under his arm he held the leather portfolio containing the missing pages. He stopped on the sidewalk and held up a finger to let Jenna know he would only be a minute, but also to offer reassurance that everything was fine.

Jenna guessed he was talking to his buyer. She tried reading his lips, but before she could make out a single word, Neal ended the call and continued toward the car.

He threw the portfolio in the back seat, and climbed behind the wheel. "That went well," he said as he started up the car. He seemed perfectly calm.

"You think it went *well?*" Jenna asked. "Feel the palm of my hand; it's all clammy from what just happened in there."

Neal playfully pushed her hand away. "I'm not going to touch your clammy hand. Stop being so dramatic." He buckled his seatbelt and then turned to her. "Any second thoughts?"

"Yes, Neal. Since you asked, I'm reevaluating my entire relationship with you. Hope all of your previous actions can withstand my revisionist scrutiny."

"You know what I meant, Jenna. Any second thoughts about the authenticity of the pages?"

"If I had any second thoughts I wouldn't have authenticated them in the first place."

"Perfect. That's exactly what I wanted to hear."

Jenna turned around in her seat. She grabbed the leather portfolio and pulled it into the front with her.

"What are you doing?" her brother asked.

She set the case on her lap, and then buckled her seatbelt. "You've got to be kidding with that question, brother. Up in that fourth-floor motel room was all business. Now comes the pleasure."

With a gleeful smile on her face, she pulled one of the pages out of the leather satchel as Neal peeled out and away.

CHAPTER 15

WHEN THE VIRGINIA RAILWAY EXPRESS docked at Broad Run Station, George and two dozen commuters boarded. He took the second car and saw an empty seat, but chose to stand instead. He needed to burn some of the nervous energy in his legs.

As the train started up, he patted his shirt pocket and felt the business card of the organ transplant network. He had yet to read the name the doctor had written inside the fold. Maybe because he wasn't sure what to do next.

George certainly didn't want to ambush the recipient with his sudden spiritual curiosity. But he was obsessed with what his wife would think of the man living off of her heart. He also was convinced that it was his responsibility to be the conduit to express her approval. Or disapproval.

Carri had always lived as if there were only twelve hours in a day. And in her eyes, most people were simply floating through life without any deep thoughts, measurable accomplishments, or emotional attachments. George never realized how much her thoughts had attached themselves to his own synapses. Now, months after her death, her negative opinions on the rest of humanity permeated his indecisive thoughts.

The train continued north toward the city, and George decided to remember this moment. He looked all around him, at the passing scenery, the faces of the passengers crowding the car, even the leather strap he was holding for balance. He wanted to remember because, after countless days of mourning over his wife, he had finally decided to visit and get to know the only part of her that was still alive. He hoped Carri would approve of his choice. But George had just enough sane brain cells left to know it didn't matter. If he didn't start living, then he might as well rip Carri's heart out of the recipient's chest and jump into the afterlife with her.

———

AS NEAL DROVE BACK TOWARD THE HIGHWAY, Jenna pulled the eighth missing page of the Codex Gigas from the leather portfolio. It barely fit on her lap. She caressed its plastic cover and admired the capital letter illumination, the unique self-taught calligraphy, the mysterious words coded in Hildegard of Bingen's "unknown language."

She wondered why the scribe had encrypted only the keywords and not the entire Latin passage. And the fact that a Benedictine abbess had created the secret language by divine inspiration only deepened the mystery.

"So who text-messaged you?" Neal asked from out of nowhere.

"What?"

"Earlier at the motel?"

"Oh, it was just Mom."

"Mom texted you?" Neal said.

Jenna could have slapped her forehead she felt so stupid; she had forgotten her mother didn't know how to text. "No, I meant she left a voicemail. She wanted to know if we were still coming tonight."

"Then let's call her, shall we?" Neal dialed the number on his phone and waited for their mother, Ruth, to pick up.

"Hey, Mom, guess who I have with me right now? Yep. She says she got your message."

Neal smiled sideways at Jenna as he listened to Ruth. "Really, Mom, you have no clue what message she's talking about? Well then, why don't we let you talk to her? Here..." He handed his phone to Jenna. "Say hello to Mom," Neal said, still smiling that weird sideways smile.

Jenna took the phone from him, thinking, *Crap.* "Hi, Mom."

"Hi, dear. You're still coming tonight, aren't you?"

"I'm not sure anymore. It's entirely up to Neal."

"If you don't come tonight, then when? Neal said you're catching the morning plane back to London."

"Well, Mother, I've been trying to reschedule that flight. So... how are you?"

"Did Neal tell you that I fired Rene?" Ruth asked. "Some things turned up missing and I'm certain she's the one who's been helping herself."

"Oh, Mother, are you sure? You're always misplacing stuff. I'd hate to think you fired your nurse because of your own—"

"I'm not senile, Jenna, not yet. And not for at least a few more years."

Jenna didn't respond. "Neal," she said, "what the hell? Weren't you supposed to turn there?" She pointed back at the onramp. "Aren't you taking the highway back into the city?"

In the background, Ruth said, "What highway? I swear, Jenna, you accuse me of being senile..."

"Don't worry about it," Neal replied. "At this hour we're way better off taking the scenic route. You'll see."

"What's going on with you, Neal? You never take the scenic route. And that includes when you were lead trombone in the high school band, walking the Grey Days Parade."

"Is your brother all right?" their mother asked.

Neal chuckled at Jenna's joke.

"Yeah," Jenna said, "he's just acting as if he's the one with jet lag."

"Well, you keep an eye on him please. I think there could be something wrong after his accident."

"His scratches are healing fine," Jenna said.

"No, I'm not talking about the scratches. I'm talking about the several minutes he was unconscious."

"What are you talking about?" Jenna asked. Her question prompted Neal to look over at her.

Ruth said, "He told me he called you when it happened. You mean to tell me that he didn't?"

"He said he didn't want to worry me."

"Jenna, give me the phone." Neal said, glancing from her to the road. He extended his hand and said, "Give it to me."

He looked more than serious, so Jenna shrugged and handed it over. She thought he planned to say something to their mother, perhaps to reprimand her or to affirm that she was, indeed, senile, but instead he clicked a button on the phone.

"Did you just hang up?!" Jenna said. "You know, I wasn't done talking to her."

"I wouldn't have let you talk to her at all if I thought she would bring up the accident."

"Yeah, about that. Why didn't you tell me you were unconscious for several minutes?"

"Why did you tell me it was Mom who texted you?"

Jenna hesitated. Her brother had specifically instructed her not to link herself to the Codex Gigas, and yet she had sent a text message that could triangulate the exact motel where the deal had gone down. It was about as stupid as parking a car with diplomatic plates at the scene of the crime.

Neal pulled the car up to a stop sign, where the intersecting road ran parallel to the Virginia Railway.

"Look, Neal, I'm not going to lie to you anymore. The text was from my co-host, Raymond. I didn't want to tell you because... big brothers can be too protective. And besides, it had nothing to do with what we're doing."

Neal contemplated it a moment. "Are you telling me the truth, Jenna? Because right now is the time for the unvarnished truth." He turned the BMW onto the road running beside the railway.

"Neal, where are you going?"

He looked in his rearview, and, calmly, he said, "Someone's following us."

Jenna stared at him a second, at those cuts on his face, and then she turned around in her seat. A silver car was slowing down at the stop sign about two hundred yards back.

"Oh my God, Neal, are you sure?" She quickly stuffed the Codex page back in the leather portfolio.

"Actually," her brother said, "I need to talk to you about my own unvarnished truth. When I had my accident, I wasn't just unconscious... I was dead."

Jenna sat up in her seat.

In the distance, a train whistled. She barely heard it.

"You died?"

"Yes, but the Angel of Light sent me back to the living. He said I still have work to do."

Her brother's voice sounded odd, as if he were channeling someone else's words.

Then with a lurch in acceleration, he swerved off the road, into a grassy field.

"What are you doing?!" Jenna screamed. She braced herself on the dash as she bounced, long hair lashing around her head. The portfolio started to slide off of her lap.

Neal accelerated toward the railway, up and over a small embankment. He hit the incline at the perfect angle and speed, so that the driver's side of the car landed between the rails, and the passenger side landed on the edge of the railroad ties.

Without missing a beat, he hit the accelerator, maxing out at fifty miles an hour on the rocky terrain. The car sounded like a helicopter as its tires treaded the beams, jostling Jenna so badly she felt concussed.

The train whistle sounded again in the near distance.

Jenna reached over to grab her brother, but the seatbelt stopped her short. She reached for the belt lock, but missed; she couldn't steady her hand as the car shuddered.

As the double-decker train became visible about half a mile away, Neal said, "The Angel of Light will illuminate you."

———

GEORGE WAS REACHING INTO HIS shirt pocket for the business card when movement in the last car caught his attention.

He squinted, wishing for better eyesight. His prescription for contact lenses had expired years ago. "But why get new ones?" he once said to his wife. "I've got 20/20 squinting."

George guessed that, with age, even his squinting was getting worse, because what he saw in the other car didn't make sense.

He saw a woman. The only person in that section of the train. She stood with her back to him, so he couldn't see her face. But she wore the same clothes and Redskins cap as Carri on the day she died.

George started toward the last car, balancing with the motion of the train. He kept his eyes on the woman as he stumbled around the other passengers, afraid that if he lost sight of her, the woman would vanish back into the ether.

He threw open the doors between the cars and passed through. The woman was in the process of sitting down, but at an angle, so it was always her back that faced him.

His wife's Christmas present, the digital camera, dangled from its cord around his neck. It bounced off of George's chest a few times but he ignored the sharp pain.

He reached for the woman and almost touched her...

And then the train squealed and braked.

George was thrown off his feet and he landed in the center aisle, right beside the woman. He looked up, and her smile dawned upon him from beneath the cap, emitting the warmest of light, so soothing he lingered on the verge of laughter and tears. And longing.

"Carri," he said.

Then the train crashed and everything went dark.

CHAPTER 16

INSTINCTIVELY, ETAN WAITED at the stop sign to watch the train hit the car. And here he had been following along behind them, debating how best to neutralize his targets and acquire the Black Pages, how best not to fail.

At first, he couldn't figure out why the driver was crossing the grassy strip. Maybe to escape the silver rental car following him? Or more likely, he was preparing to remove his bed-haired partner.

But then, as the BMW flew up onto the tracks and rocketed toward the train, Etan remembered what his employer had told him years ago: that the Black Pages were special; they had been touched by the Angel of Light. And around them good and evil would collide.

Etan put his car in gear and chased the BMW in the field. His seatbelt pinned his body back as he hit every bump and bush. He didn't know what he planned to do. Intercede somehow? Save the pages from destruction? Both were ridiculous to consider, which became clearer and clearer as he caught up. More likely he would get sideswiped by the wreckage.

So he braked. And as he did, the passenger leapt out of the BMW ahead of him; her body tumbled away from the tracks and was swallowed whole in the weeds.

A few seconds later, the train and BMW butted heads. Even from a distance Etan felt the concussion—it hit him center mass. The explosion of metal and glass nearly deafened him.

The BMW, compacted to half its size, rocketed into the air. It landed on its wheels and burst into flames.

The collision had forced the train backward, up into itself, and the rear of the locomotive jackknifed into the air as the other cars lifted it by the hitch. The locomotive and two other cars fell to opposite sides of the track, sliding and scraping and sparking along the rocks, so that only the fourth and fifth cars remained on the rails, their front ends flattened from the pileup.

As the train settled into smoke and flames, the survivors inside began to scream.

Etan raced from his rental car toward the BMW, shielding himself from the heat. Through the shattered windows he saw cloaks of black smoke bursting into fireballs.

Strangely, the airbags had not deployed, yet the engine block practically sat in the front seat. Etan saw only a vague outline of the driver, twisted and exploded and sizzling against the hot parts. He didn't see the Black Pages.

Driven back by a flare of heat and the stink of burning shit and flesh, Etan stumbled a safe distance before collapsing into the grass and weeds. People were still screaming in the train, a chorus of hoarse and piercing cries audible over the various infernos. Etan joined the choir, letting the sound mortally rip him.

After two endless years, he had failed.

Raging, Etan got to his feet and marched toward the clump of weeds where the young woman had fallen. She probably had died, but he didn't care for probabilities. A trail of blood and moans led him into the weeds where she lay, badly scratched and bruised, and still bleeding with every pulse. She looked up at him, eyes half-closed.

"I will get you help," Etan said. "Where are the pages?"

She blinked several times and began to lose focus. Etan straddled her, taking care not to weigh heavily on her chest. "Where are the pages from the Devil's Bible? I know you had them."

She stared up at the sky, into space. He was losing her. Etan clamped his hand around her throat. "Once more, the pages: where are they?"

The woman's face, already covered with scratches and splotches of blood, began to turn red as Etan throttled her neck. He let up so that she could answer his question.

"Where are the pages?!"

The grass rustled behind Etan. He turned—right into a huge rock. The blow knocked him off the woman, into a bush. He tried to stand, but fell onto one knee.

His assailant kicked him in the chest and Etan sprawled over the bush, onto hard dirt.

He rolled over and fumbled for the rooster claw necklace. Still there. Still intact.

Sweat poured into his left eye as he stood, and then he wiped it and realized it wasn't sweat, it was blood.

His attacker was in his thirties, blond. Soot and sweat covered his body. Soot and sweat, but no sign of injury from the wreck.

The man looked athletic, but not the kind of guy who played basketball. More like rugby. Which said everything about his weaknesses and strengths. The man instinctively checked for the camera that hung around his neck, and Etan used the opportunity to pull up his pant leg and snatch a small gun from his ankle holster. But when he looked up, his attacker had vanished in the grass. Distant sirens approached.

Etan glanced around, took a few shaky steps. *Forget about it*, he thought. The pages were gone.

He scrambled toward his rental car, stumbling here and there over mounds of grass. He kept watch for the blond cameraman, fully expecting another attack.

When he got to his car and climbed in, Etan checked his dirty face in the mirror. The blood had pooled primarily in his left eye socket. His green eye, unaffected, stared back at him.

Etan strapped on his seatbelt with one hand as he started the engine. In less than a minute he had returned to the road.

He grabbed some Kleenex from the glove compartment and mopped up the tears and the blood and the grime. He had cleaned everything but his nose by the time the first fire truck raced past, followed by one too many cops.

CHAPTER 17

D R. FINCHER WALKED UP INDEPENDENCE AVENUE past the Capitol Building and its wooded estate, playing "Who's the Whacko?" He had invented the game as a brain teaser in graduate school. The rules were simple: from amongst a crowd of ordinary people, he had to pick out the sociopath.

Recently all of the major newspapers had released the statistic that, in the United States, an estimated one percent of the population hid some form of psychopathy under their normal human skin. Dr. Fincher believed the study grossly underestimated the true number. He had interviewed and studied violent convicts for most of his career, and several popular periodicals had published his results. The major medical journals, however, had rejected his work.

At this point in his life, he had gone beyond just interviewing convicts and simply confirming with his tests the overwhelming genetic component to their aberrant behavior. He liked to believe he could see behind the masks psychopaths put on every day. And if he ever feared he was losing at his own game, all he had to do was glance at his reflection in a tinted window or the mirror of a parked car. There was nothing like a built-in ringer to ensure he would always win the game.

Just after Bartholdi Park and the U.S. Botanical Garden, with its steel-framed atrium domes, Dr. Fincher watched a taxi pull to the curb for an elderly woman. A young man wearing a local college sweatshirt stepped in front of her and stole the cab for himself.

Fincher smiled. On the PCL-R diagnostic test, a psychopathy checklist, two of the measured tendencies were poor behavioral control and a lack of empathy. Of course, the young man's act could have been nothing more than boorish behavior, but Fincher liked to think it was the first sign of a developing psychosis.

Ever since his early research in the prisons, he had been developing the theory that if every human could trace their DNA to a particular ancestor ape, then all psychopathy could be traced back to the Angel of Light. He had shared his theory with only two people, but never with the Angel himself. In fact, Fincher refrained from contemplating it at all while in the angel's presence, uncertain of the sanctity of his own thoughts.

The secrecy was a challenge for him, because Fincher would have given anything to administer the PCL-R test to the Angel of Light. Undoubtedly Wolfenson would score a perfect forty, if he took the test seriously and honestly. And God only knew what an fMRI would reveal about the envoy's brain.

Tucked in the pocket of Fincher's coat, a throwaway cell phone disturbed his game. He withdrew the phone and immediately answered.

138

"Yes?"

"The two targets are down," a female voice replied.

"Excellent," Fincher said. He quickly disassembled the phone, then crushed the computer chip beneath his shoe. He deposited the remains of the device in two different garbage cans along the way.

Years after his prison studies, Dr. Fincher had discovered a congregation of people exhibiting the same psychopathic traits as the inmates. They called themselves the "Red Veil," a secret society dedicated to ushering in the Angel of Light. After joining the group, Fincher quickly became a rising star in their ranks.

He had been the one to suggest that the Angel of Light would possess someone in medicine, military, politics, or business. He never explained why, but he knew the traits of a psychopath were highly desirable and successful in those fields. For instance, in politics, arrogance, ruthlessness and a lack of social conscience could get a man elected to the U.S. Senate.

This revelation had led the group to newly appointed Envoy of the Middle East, John Wolfenson. According to Dr. Fincher's preliminary research, the envoy suffered from narcissistic personality disorder, NPD; the so-called "God complex." Based on this finding, along with other compelling evidence, Dr. Fincher had determined that John Wolfenson would, indeed, be the host for the Angel of Light. From there it had all been a question of timing.

Fincher arrived at his doctor's office without spotting a single bona fide sociopath. In Washington D.C., that outcome was a shocking rarity.

A nurse checked his weight and took a blood sample while he stared at the parquet wood floor. She was pulling the needle out of his arm when Dr. Wang entered.

"Dr. Fincher," Wang said. "How are we doing today?"

"Never better."

"I apologize if I'm wrong, but I believe you were admiring the floors of this office."

"Yes, doctor, you caught me. I was just thinking how nice hardwood floors would look in my new apartment."

"That's right," Dr. Wang said, "you came here from New York. Well I only mention it because it was my father who's responsible for the wood floors you see before you."

"Your father installed these?" Fincher asked.

"Well, not exactly. Dad had already retired by the time I opened this office. But you can bet he supervised the installation."

Dr. Fincher looked down at the floor and shook his head with admiration. "Impressive is all I can say."

"I could get the number of the flooring company for you, if you'd like."

"Well," Fincher said, rather pleased with himself, "if they were good enough for your father... they're definitely good enough for me. That would be great." He was always honing his ability to bait people until they volunteered the information he sought. In a situation like this, it was harmless, but it was fulfilling to know he still had the ability.

"I'll have our receptionist get you the number."

The nurse noted something on Dr. Fincher's chart and then handed it to Dr. Wang. "Doctor Fincher weighs 175 pounds," she announced.

"That's good, right?" Fincher asked.

"Yes, you haven't gained or lost any weight," said the nurse. "One seventy-five is very good." With that, she left the two doctors alone.

"I just walked here from my office on C Street," Fincher said proudly. "Didn't even look at a cab."

"That's fantastic." Dr. Wang raised his stethoscope to his ears and applied the cold diaphragm to Fincher's back. "Any shortness of breath on the walk?"

"None. I told you I feel great."

The doctor listened in silence for half a minute before asking, "Any fever recently?"

Dr. Fincher shook his head.

"Any feeling of general fatigue?"

"Back to my usual workload, no problems."

Dr. Wang withdrew the stethoscope and made some notes on Fincher's chart. He wasn't smiling, but he also didn't look concerned.

"How is your urine output?"

"I'm still going all the time. I have to take a bathroom break every couple of hours."

"That's a good sign. A reduction in urine output is what to look out for."

With a flourish of his pen, Dr. Wang made his final note and then smirked. "Who said doctors make the worst patients?"

When they finished, Dr. Fincher visited the front desk to get the number of the flooring company. The nurse who usually sat there to collect his co-pay stood in the waiting room with a patient and another member of Dr. Wang's staff. They were all glued to the flat-screen TV, which aired a breaking news story, an aerial shot of emergency crews surrounding a train wreck.

Dr. Fincher felt adrenaline shoot through him.

It happened, he thought, *exactly as planned.*

———

ALTHOUGH HE HAD WALKED to his doctor's office, Fincher hailed a cab to Wolfenson Enterprises, too impatient to walk.

As he exited the elevator on the tenth floor, he expected the reception area to be vacant, which it was. In the conference room down the hall, a dozen of the consulting firm's employees stood around the massive TV. Fincher joined them, but cautioned himself not to grin as he soaked up their reactions.

When the receptionist saw him enter the room, she immediately headed back to her desk. The other employees looked uncomfortable as well, and Dr. Fincher began to wonder why. What had the news report revealed?

The company accountant quickly swept away his fear. "Have you been watching this?" he asked Fincher. "The Manassas Line apparently hit a car."

"A car? Are you kidding me?!"

One of the firm's secretaries said, "They just interviewed a passing motorist who saw a car fly off the tracks."

"The car was *on the tracks?*" Dr. Fincher shook his head and moved closer to the TV.

While he had been walking back from Dr. Wang's office, the reporters had updated the story. The news crawl at the bottom of the screen reported 129 casualties and five survivors being treated at the scene of the accident.

"I take that train every month to visit my wife's parents in Fairfax," one of the firm's executives said.

Dr. Fincher laid a comforting hand on his shoulder. The executive had made the crash all about himself, which was a normal initial reaction, usually followed by empathy for the bereaved families—but Fincher doubted the executive would ever get there.

Wolfenson had hired a good staff.

The reporter at the wreck finished interviewing a spokesperson for the fire department and turned to someone from the local police. "Can you give us any more information on the driver of the car that collided with the train?" she asked.

More microphones appeared out of nowhere as the policeman answered. "We do not have an ID on the driver yet, but we can confirm that there were no passengers in the vehicle at the time of the collision..."

The spokesperson kept speaking, but Dr. Fincher had calmly excused himself from the conference room. He walked to his office, where he could watch privately—and phone the envoy to alert him. But Wolfenson was already there, seated in one of his chairs and watching the news coverage.

Dr. Fincher shut the door behind him. "The news is reporting only one person in the vehicle that struck the train."

Wolfenson stared at the TV screen. "It's been my experience that the media seldom gets anything right, except for the makeup and hair."

Dr. Fincher sat down at his computer and searched for different news coverage of the accident.

"Perhaps the sister died outside of the car and no one has recovered her body," Wolfenson suggested, still staring at the footage of emergency workers tending to the wreckage and the injured.

"I guess it's possible," Fincher said.

"I suggest you send someone to check, preferably someone who knows what the young woman looks like."

"Yes, sir, of course. I will get right on it."

Wolfenson stood up. "I suspect the Landlord is behind this. That is, if the woman is alive." As he walked across the room to leave, he said, "I will be next door, waiting for the President to call."

Fincher muted the television. "What's that, sir? Did you say the President of the United States?"

Wolfenson nodded. "He's going to ask me to take a trip. I will need you to come along."

Before Fincher could say anything, or even process what he had just heard, Wolfenson left.

On TV, the train accident was interrupted by the news anchor back at the station. Fincher unmuted the set, hoping for an update. "Pam, I'm sorry to cut you off, but we have another late breaking story…"

The development was so fresh, the anchor had to abandon the teleprompter to read the report from a computer screen imbedded in her dais. "Apparently, an earthquake has struck the country of Syria. Early reports have the quake measuring 8.7 on the Richter scale."

Dr. Fincher sat up in his chair, stimulated again by a few shots of adrenaline. He listened attentively as the anchor described the unimaginable destruction, and he knew the train wreck and the earthquake were somehow linked. Not that one had caused the other, but that perhaps the stars had finally aligned.

———

A LITTLE BEFORE 5 P.M., Dr. Fincher caught the company car service to his apartment in Bethesda, Maryland. He wanted only to nap, but first he planned to pack his bags for the trip with Wolfenson. Their plane would leave for the Middle East later that evening, and he still needed to tie up a dozen loose ends beforehand.

As he entered the lobby of his apartment building, the security guard greeted him.

"There's a man who's been waiting over there for about an hour," the guard said. "He says he needs to speak to you."

In the waiting area, Fincher saw a stocky blond man with a very intense gaze, minimized by his sports shirt and jeans.

"Thank you," Dr. Fincher said, "I'll handle this." He tapped the security guard's shoulder, confirming that he carried his usual side arm.

As Fincher approached, the blond man got up and extended his hand.

"Can I help you?" Fincher asked.

"Well, to be honest, it was my wife that helped you. My name is George Wyatt."

Dr. Fincher was confused but shook George Wyatt's hand anyway, finding strength there, and something unresolved.

CHAPTER 18

G EORGE WYATT AWOKE in the aisle in the last car of the train. From a crack in the ceiling, a narrow beam of sunlight shined down on his face.

The digital camera rested on his chest, still powered on, and as he began to stir, he discovered that it aligned perfectly with the angle of his body.

Slowly, gingerly, with labored breathing, he touched all around his body. As he performed his medical check, George witnessed all of his actions through the viewfinder. He theorized that perhaps he had hit his head in the accident, because as he watched all of his movements through the camera, he never once thought it was odd.

He didn't seem to be injured.

George looked up to the seat where he had spotted his wife. It was empty now; she had somehow vanished. And yet George didn't feel troubled by that realization.

A flicker in the camera's viewfinder caught his eye. He could see a woman's face on the screen, distant and indefinite in the smoke, but distinct enough that he could make out an impish grin.

The image drove George to his feet, but he instantly had to catch himself on one of the seats.

Choking on the heavy pollution of burning machinery, upholstery, and electrical wire, George coughed and hacked but stumbled forward. He found an emergency window, clearly marked by a few shafts of in-coming light. George pulled the tab on the seal around the windowpane and then removed the glass so he could crawl outside.

He fell to the rocks, which lay like brimstone under rails and ties. Flames licked here and there as large shapes materialized in the hazy landscape. The shapes resolved even further, and George discovered the train, derailed, except for his car and the car ahead of it. Passenger seats littered the tracks. So did the passengers.

Someone began to scream.

The sound seemed to come from somewhere beyond the derailed lo-comotive, but as George hurried toward it, he thought it could also just be the ringing in his ears, or the creaking of metal and the hissing of steam.

And then he heard the scream again in the percussions and trebles of wreckage.

George scrambled down the dirt embankment, out into the grass, which lashed at his waist and higher.

The smell of cooking flesh poured off a BMW burning nearby. He knew without knowing that the car had collided with the train.

He lost himself in the tangled growth and circled around, trying to find the woman he had glimpsed through his camera.

George paused along the way to pick up a large rock. He didn't question why; it felt ordained.

In a clearing he encountered a man straddling a woman, garroting her, and this, too, seemed fated.

He knew without seeing her that she was the woman with the impish grin.

She wasn't moving.

George charged forward with such clear decisiveness that he barely expended any energy or strength. He hit the man with the rock, and the man fell, and then George kicked him and drove him back. The woman wasn't moving, not even to breathe.

Hide! Carri cried out to him, and her voice in George's head startled him so badly that he ducked in the grass.

Sirens began to sing their song in the distance, and soon George sensed the attacker moving away. He peeked over the weeds and saw the man running for his car.

George crawled over to the sandy-haired woman and probed her neck for a pulse. At his very touch, she coughed and gasped and labored for air.

"Are you all right?" George asked.

"I think... I think..."

You need to leave, Carri whispered. *Both of you—now.*

The sirens drew closer as he helped the woman to her feet. He let her use him as a crutch, and they hobbled toward the nearby woods.

"Wait," the woman said, stopping so suddenly they almost toppled. "We have to... get something..."

Clenching her jaw with the effort, she led George through the weeds to a place near the tracks; she went right there as if she, too, knew something she shouldn't, and there in the dirt lay a leather portfolio.

CHAPTER 19

THE CUTS ON NEAL'S FACE burst into blood as he sped toward the train.

Jenna threw open her door and held it open, but her seatbelt caught her. She reached for the release, accidentally smashing the leather portfolio over the button.

Neal slapped her hand away. His blood, in the bounding of tires over ties, dribbled, bounced, and flung everywhere in fat drops, as if he were being shaken apart at the seams. He never took his eyes off the train.

Jenna tried again for the release, and this time succeeded; her seatbelt retracted and she fell toward the open door, but Neal caught her by the meat of the arm and pulled her back. She retaliated by grabbing the steering wheel.

The car lurched in her direction and hit a rail. Neal lost his grip on Jenna's arm, and then the car bucked her out into space.

Somewhere in the rocks beneath her, the portfolio flapped like a leathered wing. Jenna hit the ground and...

Woke up in bed. Not in a hospital, but in someone else's home. The clock on the nightstand blinked midnight.

Jenna stirred, but then almost instantly held still. Dull throbbing washed over her in waves, spiked with painful abrasions from head to foot. Even the slightest movement made her want to vomit.

Jenna began to feel like she might as well have been hit by the train.

Moving only her eyes, and feeling every muscle tighten and twist, she looked around the room. She saw a TV on a dresser, a chest of drawers—and a woman across from her, staring back.

Jenna flinched, almost cried out, but then she realized it was a mirror above the chest. She didn't recognize herself, not at first glance. Earlier, she had fussed over the kink in her hair, but now her hair was matted on one side, tangled on the other.

How long had she been unconscious that her first reaction was to flinch when she saw herself?

In the mirror, Jenna noticed she was wearing another woman's nightgown. Small bandages covered her hands and face, and bruises dotted her breast and shoulders. A dark handprint marred her biceps, the mark from her brother, Neal, where he had tried to detain her in the car.

A man's voice got Jenna's attention. It was from the other room. She cocked her ear to catch what he was saying. After a few minutes, she realized she couldn't make out any of the words. At least her urge to vomit had apparently passed. And she felt as if she could actually move without dying.

Jenna sat up and rested for a moment.

Then, just as she was about to get out of bed, the man from the other room entered. She recognized him. He was the man with the camera around his neck, the same man who had saved her from the stranger with the rooster claw and the lone green eye. It should have comforted her, but it did not.

George stopped abruptly a few feet inside the room, surprised to see Jenna awake.

She surprised him again by being the first one to speak. "Tell me that this is all a nightmare."

"Funny," George said, "that's the same thing I've been waking up and saying for the past four months. I hope that the two of us aren't involved in some sort of closed timelike curve. That would really piss me off."

He saw the tears welling up in Jenna's eyes and realized he was coming off as emotionally distant, even obtuse, which wasn't his intention.

To atone for his mistake, George moved calmly to a glass of water he had placed earlier on the nightstand. He offered it to her.

Jenna shook her head.

"Come on, you've been sleeping for hours. You have to be thirsty. Think about it, would I really go to all the trouble of bringing you back here just to poison the first glass of water I offer you? Perhaps it would make sense to the man who tried to kill you, but not to me."

She was feeling incredibly dehydrated, and his argument did make logical sense. So Jenna grabbed the glass and drank. Some of the water spilled from her mouth, as even the simple act of swallowing hurt.

George backed off to the bedroom door, to give her space. He certainly didn't want to intimidate her.

Jenna set the empty glass on the nightstand right next to the framed photograph of him and his wife. Carri had taken the picture herself, holding the camera out and away to capture their tight embrace.

"Do you think you're up to some questions?" George asked.

"Not really. But I might be up to asking you a few. Let's start with 'where am I?'"

"You're in my apartment."

"Why?"

"Because it was the only place I could think to bring you after the accident."

"Ever heard of a hospital?"

"No hospitals. My wife told me to bring you here."

"Your wife?" Jenna said. She glanced at the nightstand, at the woman in the photograph.

"She's dead," George replied.

"Oh my God, in the train wreck?" Jenna felt a sharp pang of guilt. Had her brother killed this man's wife?

George held up his hand to calm her down. "She told me to get you away from the accident. I think she was concerned that the authorities would ask you questions, and she knew we don't really have time for that."

Jenna kept nodding, though she didn't fully understand how this man's wife could have told him anything, if she died in the wreck. "What's your name?" she asked.

"George Wyatt. And yours is Jenna Grant."

"How did you know that?"

"I already told you. Would you like more water?"

She didn't respond.

From the bedroom dresser, George picked up a remote control and turned on the TV. For an instant, the footage of the earthquake in Aleppo, Syria, looked vaguely like a train wreck, because the camera had been zoomed in on some ambiguous devastation and smoke. But then it zoomed out, and George flipped through a few channels until he found coverage of the actual train wreck. He muted the sound and let Jenna watch in silence.

Train cars lay crushed and burning on either side of the tracks, and paramedics were helping survivors: dressing wounds, carrying people in gurneys. All the news footage seemed blurry, jumpy, and chaotic.

In the corner of the screen, the network had posted a DMV photograph of Neal, the Neal Jenna remembered before this trip to the States, the one without the cuts. It should have angered her, or made her cry, but she didn't feel anything—couldn't.

"Look," she said, "I know you don't know my brother, but... believe me, it wasn't him who did this. Not really. Actually, not in a million years. He couldn't have done this. Not any of this."

"I understand." George tried his best to look like he truly empathized. "But nobody else would understand, and that's why we left the scene of the crime."

It wasn't lost on Jenna that he hadn't said "accident."

"We also left because the people who are behind your brother's actions are going to cause more death and destruction."

"Wait..." Jenna said, alarmed. But she couldn't finish the thought; the sudden tension in her muscles triggered fresh waves of pain, and she collapsed onto the bed.

George moved toward her but didn't get very far. She held up her hand, a gesture that was so emphatic, she might as well have planted her palm against his chest. He instantly halted.

Jenna clinched her eyelids tight enough to squeeze out new tears, and when she finally opened them, she couldn't say how long they had been closed. George hadn't moved. He looked like a statue, waiting to come to life if given the right sign.

"Are you...?" Jenna said.

George began to move. "Am I what?"

"One of them. Whoever's behind what happened to my brother."

"No, I'm not. At least I don't think so." He didn't sound at all reassuring. "I know that Neal... your brother, had you examine pages from a medieval document—"

"How? How could you possibly know that if you weren't involved?"

George took a step toward the bed, but then thought better of it and took one step back. "Because," he said, "I saw what you had done with your brother. I saw these things shortly after the wreck, before I woke up."

Jenna just stared at him. For the first time, she thought maybe she had suffered a concussion or some sort of injury to her brain, because very little of what this man was saying made any sense. "You mean in a dream?" Jenna asked.

"Sort of."

Using the remote control, he unmuted the TV and turned up the volume. The news had moved to another story, and the anchor behind the desk was saying something about the latest development in the possible murder of a French diplomat.

The broadcast switched to a shot of a news reporter, standing in the parking lot of a seedy motel.

"Oh my God," Jenna said quietly.

"Frank," the reporter began, "I'm standing in front of the Real Comfort Motel where just a few minutes ago authorities have positively identified the two bodies discovered in a fourth-floor room. They have confirmed that one of the bodies is Arnaud Tottone, French Ambassador to the United States. The other body is Henri Turiaf, who authorities have confirmed was Tottone's personal bodyguard and an employee of the French embassy in Washington, D.C. The guard appears to have been shot with his own gun, which was then turned on the French Ambassador."

As the reporter continued his story, the screen filled with images of Tottone and Turiaf.

George muted the TV. "You met these men, didn't you? They were the ones who had the document you examined?"

"Why didn't they mention the blonde?" Jenna asked, watching the news as if expecting to see the woman's body, or at least her mug shot. "Did my brother kill these men? Or did she?"

"It doesn't matter," George said.

"It does to me."

He tossed the remote onto the bed and walked closer to her. She clenched her fists just in case this was the moment he chose to confront

157

her. As soon as he saw her reaction, he stopped. But he still asked what he needed to know.

"Do you remember anything unusual your brother might have said before he died?"

Jenna thought about it.

When she didn't immediately respond, George tried to rephrase his question. "Was there anything he might have said that didn't sound like the person you knew?"

Everything since waking up at The Willard seemed like a dream to her, like maybe she was still sleeping. Fog blurred her memories, and everything came back in echoes and streaks. Worse, she couldn't focus on one thing. Her mind kept drifting back to the pain.

"He did say one thing," she finally recalled. "That he'd died, and... something like... the Angel of Light had brought him back."

George didn't visibly react to what she said. Jenna couldn't tell whether or not he had heard the phrase before.

"You need to know that the people who controlled your brother are still out there," he told her. "And they're now looking for you."

"Why?"

"I'm not sure why, but—" He coughed, cleared his throat, and tried again. "It has to do with... the document—"

He continued to cough.

As he hunched over, eyes shut, Jenna tried to get out of bed. She needed to move, needed to pace. Or run away. She didn't know which. But again, a jolt of pain pinned her to the mattress.

Clenching her teeth, Jenna threw the covers aside and got out of bed.

George didn't notice her getting up until he was done coughing and he had dried his eyes.

"You're up," he said. "That's great—" The last word turned into another coughing fit, much deeper in his chest than before. He felt the pressure behind his eyes and in his face, a hot, red swelling. And then he coughed so hard that he sprayed blood onto the bottom of the bedspread.

"Oh my God!" Jenna said, turning away.

George stared at the red drops for a few moments, feeling nothing but the burn in his throat and chest. Then he walked into the adjoining bathroom and turned on the faucet.

Luckily, the rush of water concealed the creaking of floorboards as Jenna hobbled toward the bedroom door. She glanced at the bathroom, as if any moment George might spring out and catch her. He hadn't shut himself in, and she could see him bent over the sink.

Jenna made it to the bedroom door and peered out at the living room and dining room, scanning for anyone else who might be in the apartment. She spotted the leather portfolio on George's dinner table.

The tabletop, although long and wide, barely accommodated the eight pages of the Codex Gigas spread out.

This was what her brother had almost killed her for, this document. This was what all of those people on the train had died for. She just didn't know why.

She *needed* to know why.

Jenna moved toward the bathroom, where George was still hunched over the sink, coughing and spitting and watching the water wash blood down the drain.

"Are you all right?" Jenna asked him. She leaned in the doorway for the support. When he didn't answer, she said, "Why don't you see a doctor?"

"Because he'll just... tell me what I already know."

Jenna didn't have the energy to ask what he meant. So she waited for him to finish his thought.

George finally stopped coughing and sprinkled some water on his face. Slowly, he looked up to stare at his reflection. When he spoke, it was in such a disembodied voice that Jenna actually thought he was talking to himself.

"I should have died in the train wreck. But something happened and now I'm somehow standing here." He turned to her reflection in the mirror. "I don't believe I have more than a few days. So that's not much time to figure out why I'm still alive. And it's not much time to figure out what I'm supposed to do to help you."

Normally, Jenna processed information quickly and could form an opinion just as fast. But now she could barely process what had happened within the last twenty-four minutes, let alone the last twenty-four hours. Nothing made sense anymore.

"Help me do what?" she asked.

George reached into his pocket and pulled out a folded business card. He held it out to Jenna, so she could see the name on the back. "Do you know this man?" he asked.

Jenna shook her head. She had never heard of Dr. Colin Fincher.

160

CHAPTER 20

"I'M SORRY, I'M NOT FOLLOWING YOU," Dr. Fincher said. He and George Wyatt stood in the lobby of Fincher's apartment building. Fincher looked genuinely confused.

"You did receive a heart transplant about four months ago, correct?" George asked.

"I... why, yes, of course I did. Are you saying it was your wife who donated the heart?"

"Yes, my wife, Carri. She died in a car accident."

Over the last two decades, Dr. Fincher had conducted hundreds of group therapy sessions and had counseled hundreds of patients using talk therapy; he had also been a guest speaker and panelist at several conventions. He had become such a smooth talker he had forgotten how awkward speechlessness could be.

He had the urge to shake George's hand, but believed it would be interpreted as a completely underwhelming gesture. So he hugged the man.

George returned the embrace, and for a few short seconds he felt the subtle beat of Carri's heart.

The doctor released him, but kept a hand on George's shoulder. "Would you like to come upstairs for a few minutes to talk?"

"Yes," George said. "I would like that very much."

And so they went.

———

DR. FINCHER'S APARTMENT looked like something from a catalog rather than real life, minimally decorated with modern furniture and Asian art, paintings of koi fish and waves.

"So you'll have to excuse the mess," Fincher said as he hung up his coat in an entryway closet.

George had nothing to excuse. The doctor kept the apartment immaculately clean, except for one corner of the room, where two stacks of moving boxes leaned against the wall.

"I wish I could say I just moved here from New York," Fincher said, "but the truth is, I've been here for over two months and still haven't completely unpacked."

"New York," George said. "Yes, that's where I was told you lived when you received the transplant. I hope you don't mind, I had to make some phone calls to track you down."

"No, of course not. I'm glad you did. Can I get you something to drink?"

"Have you unpacked the liquor?"

Fincher smiled. "That might be the first thing I unpacked. What would you like?"

"Anything with vodka would be great."

"Coming right up."

A floor-to-ceiling window looked out on the starlight of Bethesda. Next to the window the architecture integrated a wet bar with two leather-backed stools.

Behind the bar, Dr. Fincher opened the glass door to a wall cabinet and reached for two glasses, but then hesitated and only grabbed one. As he put some ice in the glass, he asked, "How about some vodka and cranberry juice?"

George took a seat on one of the stools at the bar. "That sounds great. But aren't you going to join me?"

"Perhaps another time," said Fincher, pouring the vodka and cranberry juice into a shaker.

"See, this is what I was afraid of. You probably have a cocktail at the end of the day, but because I'm here you've decided not to."

Fincher stared at the shaker. "The reality is, your wife has given me a gift. The last thing I want to give you is the impression that I take her gift lightly."

"Well, first of all," George said, "I've come to meet you, not judge you. And second of all, my wife and I used to have at least one glass of wine every night. I bet if her heart could speak to you, it would be asking for that drink."

Dr. Fincher grinned. He got himself a glass and added more vodka and cranberry juice to the shaker. He mixed it up and then poured their drinks.

"To your wife," Fincher said.

"To Carri."

They touched glasses, with a clink and the shifting of ice. Then they each sipped their cocktail and savored the tart burn.

"Looking for the scar?" Fincher asked.

George's attention had drifted down to the doctor's blue dress shirt, to his chest; he hadn't realized how obvious he had been. "I'm sorry, I guess it did cross my mind."

"I'll tell you what," Fincher said, setting down his drink. "I'll show you my scar if you show me a picture of your wife."

George smiled. "It's a deal."

Fincher unbuttoned his shirt and pulled it open. A thick ten-inch scar ran from his sternum to the top of his stomach, like a zipper on a costume.

George could see the beat of his wife's heart caught behind the doctor's ribcage, could see the pulse of her physically move him.

Fincher said, "I guess I died during the operation."

George locked eyes with him. "Really?"

"Yes."

"Before or after the transplant?"

Fincher hesitated, wondering why it mattered. He shrugged and said, "I'm sorry, I'm not sure."

"What happened when you died?"

"Nothing. I mean, nothing I remember. They put me pretty deep under. But I guess there was a four-alarm fire in the operating room to revive me." Fincher started buttoning up his shirt. "Anyway... let's see a picture of this beautiful woman who saved my life."

George nodded and retrieved a picture of Carri from his wallet. Before he handed it to the doctor, he said, "It's a few years old. My wife, she was a photographer and pretty particular about the way light hit her in photographs. Especially in the ones I took of her."

Fincher chuckled.

George handed the picture to him, and the doctor stared at it without saying a word.

In the photo, Carri sat on a bicycle they had rented to ride around the Hamptons during a summer visit. They had been riding around all day, so a vital glow bloomed in her cheeks. Sun and shadow highlighted her muscles and curves.

George managed to finish off his cocktail before the doctor finally said, "I'm not worthy of your wife's gift." He handed the picture back to George. "You must miss her terribly."

"Yes, I do," George said. "She was an angel of light." He had waited to say it until the doctor was sipping his drink. Fincher didn't choke or accidentally spit up his cocktail, or even clear his throat. But he did stop for a microsecond as he registered the words.

George turned his eyes back to the photograph.

He wasn't sure if he had always felt this way, but now, as he stared down her subtle, knowing smile, her beauty seemed to flow from the revelation of some great mystery, one which he felt he might never know.

Suddenly, blood covered Carri's face.

"Your nose," Dr. Fincher said. "It's bleeding." He offered a cocktail napkin, and as George reached for it across the bar, he dripped on the granite countertop.

Dr. Fincher stared at the blood for several moments, at the three bright drops marring the otherwise flawless stone. "I'll be right back," he said, and he moved from behind the bar toward his kitchen. "I'll get a washcloth."

"Thanks," George said, holding the cocktail napkin up to his nose.

In the kitchen, Dr. Fincher wetted a hand towel beneath the faucet. He folded the warm, damp cloth neatly. By the time he got back to the bar, George was no longer there.

"Mr. Wyatt?" Fincher called, glancing down the hall to the bedrooms and bathroom. He didn't receive an answer. And all of the doors down the hall stood open, rooms dark.

Fincher turned and realized that the front door to the apartment hung ajar. He looked out into the hallway and saw the elevator doors closing.

Dr. Fincher frowned and returned to his bar to clean up the blood. Along with the red drops, George had left the photograph of his wife on the granite countertop.

Angel of Light, he had called her.

Fincher picked up his drink and took a sip, contemplating the mess George Wyatt had left behind.

———

GEORGE RODE THE ELEVATOR DOWN, alone except for his reflection in the mirrored paneling. His nose had stopped bleeding. His hands had begun to shake.

As the elevator opened onto the lobby, George stuffed the bloody cocktail napkin in his pocket and stepped out.

He had told Dr. Fincher that he had come solely to meet him, not judge him. George had lied. And now he felt absolutely certain the man he had just shared a drink with was somehow involved in the train accident and the attempts on Jenna's life.

George nodded to the security guard as he left the building, glad to be out of there. If he had stayed, he would have succumbed to his wife's voice in his head, which was still shouting, "Kill him, George— kill him!"

CHAPTER 21

WHEN GEORGE LEFT TO check out the name on the business card, Jenna immediately climbed out of bed. The alarm clock on the nightstand blinked midnight, so she had no clue what time it was, just that it was dark.

Before he left, George had given Jenna pain pills from an old prescription; she felt much better. Still, she moved slowly, stiffly. Some injuries were too deep to numb.

Resting awhile in the bedroom doorway, she glanced at George's dining table, where he had spread out the eight pages from the Codex Gigas. Maybe he thought if he laid it out before her like a gourmet meal she wouldn't be able to resist taking a few nibbles. But Jenna had no problem ignoring the temptation. After everything she had been through, the last thing she planned to do was ignore her instincts. Trusting her love for Neal rather than her paranoid gut had ended up getting hundreds of people killed.

Moving from the doorway, but giving the table and pages a wide birth, Jenna began to explore George's apartment. Her instincts were telling her that was the smart thing to do.

He might as well have been a Londoner, the way he decorated the place: objects piled on top of each other, books stacked on every available tabletop; the larger, thicker books piled so high they created their own tables. Jenna would have felt right at home plopping down on the couch for a meal or a good drink.

The Christmas tree, however, ruined the atmosphere. The thing had wasted away to a stick, as if inflicted with some terminal illness, still tacky with tinsel and crusts of fake snow. Jenna wondered how much she could trust someone who clung to things so obviously dead, someone who didn't even open his own Christmas presents.

She moved on to the photographs that covered the living room walls. Most had been stylishly framed, although quite a few had been simply tacked up in one corner to a bulletin board above a desk.

Some of the pictures featured George. The rest focused on Washington, D.C. Artsy shots. Like the Lincoln Memorial at sunset, and a penny held in alignment with the sun; or the Washington Memorial standing against the dark of night, quarter moon.

A digital camera sat on the desk in the corner. The same one George had worn when he'd saved Jenna from the strangler in the field. She picked it up and turned it on.

The first picture in the digital album showed a gravesite with a metal marker. Carri Wyatt's final resting place.

Jenna stared at the thumbnail for quite some time, at the year of death stamped in eternal metal.

Last year, she thought. Then it dawned on her: *Before Christmas*.

She shut her eyes and regretted her insensitive reaction to the dead tree. Carri must have died two or three months ago.

Feeling horrible, Jenna advanced to the next picture, which took her by complete surprise. She almost didn't believe what she was looking at.

Sometimes on digital cameras, she knew that if you navigated past the end of the album, it would cycle back to the beginning, to the earliest image. So at first she thought the grave marker had been the last picture, and the one she was seeing now was the first. Otherwise, how could George's wife have died before the train accident if here she was sitting on the train in a photograph taken seconds before the wreck?

Someone else in Jenna's shoes might have grabbed the disc and gone running to the tabloids, screaming, "It's a miracle! It's a miracle!" But not Jenna. For one thing, she didn't believe in miracles. She also didn't believe in the force normally attributed to them. Other than that, she rather liked reading the tabloids, especially when they ran articles about a waffle that looked exactly like the Mother Mary, or stories about a seven-year-old's squirt gun that shot the tears of Christ.

Even before she had to declare her major on a college application, Jenna had decided to study archeology. And not just because she had spent countless summers with her mother on digs and knew what to expect. History fascinated her. Especially how history was shaped. Which was why she wanted to specialize in religious artifacts.

However, when it finally came time to fill out college paperwork, Jenna had hesitated to declare archeology as her major. While she knew religion had driven countless men to erect monuments in stone, deface their bodies, and even sacrifice other human beings in the name of a higher power, she could never truly empathize with such fervor. Indeed, what she already had studied about historical religious practices almost never failed to repulse her. And yet, she did eventually write "Archeology" in the small box under "Major," with the notion that, after a few years, she could always switch her interests.

But she never did.

All throughout graduate school, and even through years and years of unearthing some of the most beautiful religious relics imaginable, Jenna never once felt the compulsion to reevaluate her lack of belief in a higher power. Her perspective had gotten her into some awkward situations. Traveling around the world had given her numerous opportunities to mingle among thousands of people celebrating their religion, and more than a few times she felt the pressure to drop to her knees in prayer like everyone else. But she always managed to hold onto her convictions and stay on her feet. It oftentimes reminded her of high school, then college, when someone was passing around a joint and Jenna was the only one in the circle who shook her head.

She set the camera on the desk and looked over at the dinner table, at the pages from the Codex Gigas.

Legend had it that the devil had written the book. She, of course, had scoffed at the notion. Now Jenna wondered if her skepticism would end up getting more people killed. Obviously some people were willing to take extraordinary measures to acquire the relic. Her brother had been willing.

She needed to know why. It was the major reason she hadn't tried to escape from George. Despite all of her suspicions, she had a nagging instinct she could trust him. Jenna suspected that perhaps he was just like her: an unsuspecting victim who had been snatched from relative obscurity and deposited onstage in a play already well into its second act.

Jenna grabbed a tablet of paper and a pencil from Carri's desk, then turned on the living room TV to a news channel—more coverage on the earthquake overseas.

With the news as background noise, she pulled up a chair at the table and glanced over the first few ancient leaves from the Codex, the laws of Benedictine monks. Nothing out of the ordinary there.

She turned her attention to the quatrains and began to translate them on the pad of paper.

It was upon the fall when the light
From the morning star came upon me
We were thusly joined in isolation
A labor of redemption and rebellion

The star claimed his light to be brief
But it blinds for eternity
Or long enough to rite this injustice
Time enough to plan an escape.

He will shine again when the stars align
Joining souls to cover his feet
Aware that his days will be numbered
With nights illuminated by his dark intent

He knows his time of deliverance
When the land is ruled by fist and storm
Swords and famine spread as locusts
And two legged beasts bring plague to the herd

From the clouds few will glimpse his eclipsed appearance
A red veil conceals the black hole in his heart
Close to death the deceived open their eyes
Moving blindly by his angelic light

Loons guide his descent
Preparing a nest for his landing
Never suspecting that the fish they gather
Will be snatched from the mouths of their own ranks

The Restrainer holds back the star
But a fatal wound invites his light
An astonished world is a witness
As a messenger of peace is resurrected

No longer bound by the gravities of the land
The Emissary prepares his flock
They will fly toward the sun
The blind and deceived trapped in their beaks

An ancient city will shake apart
And lost souls will cry in chorus
Voices heard by the wind and then by an archangel
Who will trumpet them, and they will rise

His veiled plan calls for raising nineteen
And they will cast their sleepy eyes
On the most beautiful of jewels
Rebuilding a house on shattered sacred stone

From the seed he has planted
A slithering root will grow
The serpent will be watered from oceans of blood
And fertilized by the bones of the beasts

This is the testament of our joined wills
A sunrise that blinds, nay a dark horizon which fades
One awaits the deceived
It will be a sunrise that could blind us all

A few words and phrases translated in such an odd way that Jenna wondered whether her Latin was rusty, or whether the author had intended the connotations.

Two lines in particular interested her: "Close to death the deceived open their eyes / Moving blindly by his Angelic light."

She made a note to come back to the lines later for a more nuanced translation, and then she went on to copy down the eighth and final page. She planned to work from her notebook instead of from the source material; the vellum leaves were just too large and sacred for her to constantly handle.

Jenna was hunching over the old leather page, making sure to capture the Bingen symbols precisely, when a noise in the hallway startled her.

Approaching footsteps.

Immediately she thought of the blonde from the motel. And the man with the one green eye. And her brother.

Jenna leapt to her feet, grabbed the remote control and turned off the TV set, then held her breath so she could hear. The beating of her heart didn't help.

The footsteps stopped outside the door.

George had said Neal's associates still wanted her dead. She glanced around the stacks of books for a knife or a baseball bat, or anything she could use as a weapon, cursing her own stupidity for not finding one earlier.

She heard a key slide into the lock, and then the door pushed open. She stiffened, hurting every pulled and torn muscle in her body. And then George quickly shut and locked the door behind him, and Jenna's muscles gave up so thoroughly she almost collapsed beside the table.

"You've been looking at the pages?" George said as he approached her.

Jenna didn't answer. Instead, she went over to Carri's desk and picked up the camera. "You were wearing this at the time of the train accident, right?"

George sighed. He already knew what she was going to say.

"I hope you don't mind, but I looked at the pictures on here. And actually, I kind of went through your entire apartment while you were gone, so... I hope you don't mind."

"No," George said, "I understand." From the look on his face, he seemed like he truly did not mind.

Jenna turned on the camera, which was still in album mode, displaying the final impossible picture. She held up the digital viewfinder for George. "Did you see this?"

He nodded.

"Isn't that your wife?"

George took the camera from Jenna and stared at the image. Because of a lens flare and the angle of the woman's face, a skeptic could easily contend that there wasn't sufficient proof to identify the woman as Carri. But George knew different. He recognized the smile.

"Right before the accident," he said, "I saw... Carri. I started to walk toward the train car she was sitting in, but... I didn't take this picture. The camera must have gone off somehow."

Jenna took notice of the shutter release, located on top of the camera, a hard button to trigger accidently. "Did you see your wife after the train accident?"

"No. She was gone."

"But you believe she was there on the train."

"It doesn't matter what I believe. Carri is dead. I just met the man who has her heart." George moved past her and set the camera down on the dining room table.

Jenna processed what he had said and waited for more. When he didn't follow through, she said, "Well? Aren't you going to tell me how it went?"

177

George stared down at the Codex Gigas pages. "I had a feeling before I went there that he was involved in all this. So when I was talking to him, I mentioned the phrase 'Angel of Light.'"

Jenna frowned. "That's the exact same thing my brother said."

"I know. And Dr. Fincher's reaction was... not surprising. I think he and your brother were connected."

Jenna's frown deepened. "One of the pages has a phrase in it..." She picked up her tablet of Codex translations and scanned until she found the lines. "'Close to death the deceived open their eyes/ Moving blindly from by his Angelic light.'" She looked at George. "What do you think it means?"

"Why don't you sit down," he said.

Jenna slapped the tablet on the tabletop and crossed her arms. "I've been sitting for hours. Please, just answer my question."

The power on the camera switched off and the image of George's wife faded away. He wanted to turn it back on, but he knew Jenna was only sticking around because he had answers, and he didn't want her to think he was stalling.

"I want to read what you've translated," he said, "because the same phrase came into my head the moment I woke up from the accident."

"Angel of Light," Jenna said.

"Yes."

"What does it mean?"

George hesitated, knowing how it would sound. "In the Bible, it's another name for... Satan."

Jenna pursed her lips and studied his expression. On numerous visits to the Mideast for archeological digs, she had come across more religious zealots than she cared to remember, and every single one of them, as they protested at religious sites or marched outside of foreign embassies—every single one exhibited the same glazed-eye fervor. She often worried that if some influential leader arose with the real means and desire to unite the world in peace, he'd be demonized as the Antichrist and shot.

But what she saw in George's eyes was the exact opposite of fanaticism: she saw a dull, fixed stare, almost as if he were hypnotized.

"Okay, so let me see if I've got this straight," she said. "The phrase 'Angel of Light' is really a euphemism for 'Satan.' And somehow this guy... what's his name..."

"Dr. Colin Fincher."

"Somehow this Dr. Fincher's involved with Satan because when you mentioned the phrase 'Angel of Light' his eyes twinkled. And you're connected to this because your wife, Carri... how long ago did she die?"

"Three months," George said with very little emotion.

"And that's how Fincher got her heart. So now *I'm* involved because my brother, who also used the phrase 'Angel of light,' tried to kill me with a train... the very train you just happened to be riding. So, what, this is some sort of religious Good versus Evil thing? Is that what my brother died for?"

"I know it sounds crazy," George said.

"Do you truly know how crazy? Because that would make me feel a whole lot better."

George looked at the dinner table. "You didn't mention these pages," he said, picking up her tablet of translations.

Jenna watched him carefully as he read the quatrains. If he was surprised, excited, or scared by anything in the poems, his face didn't reveal it.

"Is this everything that's on the pages?" he asked.

Jenna picked up the fourth and final Codex Gigas leaf and flipped it over to the eighth page. "I haven't translated this. It's written in modified medieval Latin, sprinkled with words from the *Lingua Ignota*."

"Excuse me? What's—"

"It means 'unknown language.' A German Benedictine abbess created it back in the twelfth century. Whoever wrote this is using her words as code."

"Can you break it?" George asked.

"Maybe. But I'd need to get some notes I made in graduate school."

"Then that's our next step," he said, putting down the pad of paper. "Where are the notes?"

"At my mother's house in Occoquan, Virginia."

George shook his head. "Your mother's house is one of the places they will be waiting."

"That may be, but the last time I spoke with my mother was in the car with my brother right before..." Jenna swallowed the rest of the sentence, and felt sick because of it. "She's got to know what he did by now. And no doubt she thinks I'm dead too. So even if my notes weren't at her house, I'd still want to go and see my mother. Understand?"

"Yes, of course," George said, again with no emotion.

The apathy really was starting to creep her out.

"But have you seen the news?" he asked. "The media has your mother's house completely surrounded. We'll have to come up with a way so no one knows who you are."

Jenna nodded and set down the leather leaf. "I think I have an idea how to make that happen. Can we go right now?"

George was still staring at the eighth page. "You said not all the words were coded. Can you understand some of the passages?"

This time it was Jenna's turn to act neutral, hoping her face didn't reveal how intrigued she had been since her cursory translation in the motel room.

"Actually," she said, "the words appear to be an exorcism."

CHAPTER 22

WHEN PATRICIA WOLFENSON entered her apartment in Dupont Circle, she heard the TV in the master bedroom and knew John was home.

Not long after their honeymoon, she had asked her husband why he kept the TV on at all times. He had looked away, embarrassed. "Before I met you," he said, "the TV was like... having someone else in the room. It just... it gets too quiet without it."

She eventually grew accustomed to the constant stream of news, stocks, and sports, but now she found it odd all over again; odd that the man claiming to be her husband would have the same aversion to being alone.

She had very little doubt that this man was an imposter, except at times like this. Hopefully Dr. Hartman would resolve the confusion.

But first, she had to figure out how to tell John to see the therapist. And she had to do it now, or she never would.

Patricia set her purse on the entryway table near a picture of their son, Scotty, taken when he was still healthy. She followed the sound of the TV to the master bedroom and stopped in the doorway when she saw John's suitcase spread out on the bed, half packed.

"John?"

A man sprang out of the bathroom, wielding something in his hand. Patricia flinched, almost jumped back, until she realized it was just John with his toiletry kit.

"Oh, hey," he said. "Didn't hear you come in."

"What's going on here?"

"Didn't you get my messages?"

"No. I must've forgotten to turn my phone back on." She had powered it off for her meeting with Dr. Hartman. "I didn't know you were going on a trip," she said.

John nodded and packed his toiletry kit in the suitcase. "The President called. He asked me to lead an official contingent to Tel Aviv."

"What? Why?"

"To gather supplies and personnel."

"For what?"

John frowned. "Haven't you seen the news? There's been an earthquake in Syria."

"Oh my God."

"It hit 8.2 in Aleppo." He pointed to the TV above the fireplace. "They've been covering it all day. Surprised you haven't seen it."

When Patricia saw the destruction in all of its high definition, she put a hand over her mouth.

Aleppo had fallen to ruins around the domes and minarets of mosques. In the background, high on a hill, the city's citadel still stood, impregnable ramparts of stone.

A caption at the bottom of the screen estimated an unimaginable death toll.

"We were just there," Patricia said, looking for familiar places through the dust and the smoke.

"Well, no, I was still brokering the peace treaty, I think. So it's been over a year."

He was right, of course, but the memories were still fresh. A year ago Aleppo had been a bustling city of souks and mosques and Christian cathedrals, one of the most ancient cities in the world; the second biggest in Syria next to Damascus: two to three million people—*nice* people.

Despite a volatile history of earthquakes and conquerors—Hittite, Assyrian, Persian, and Greek—Aleppo's citizens had been incredibly hospitable. Complete strangers often had invited Patricia to their homes for coffee or kibbeh, cracked wheat and minced lamb.

Now, many of those same people were either dead or trapped under rubble, in the dark, in the dust, screaming for help.

The news cut to a reporter, interviewing the anguished mother of two earthquake victims. "She says she'll never forgive herself," the reporter said, translating from Syrian Arabic. "She says if she hadn't been so late to pick them up, her sons would have never been in the schoolhouse when it collapsed."

The mother broke into wails and sobs, unintelligible yet easier and easier to understand. Patricia wept, remembering what it was like to be shaken so deeply, her pillars toppled, the foundation cracked.

She noticed John suddenly in the closet doorway, watching the news through his own tears. He glanced at her and then ducked into the closet, clearing his throat.

Patricia turned the volume down on the TV to silence the grieving. For a while, she listened to John rummaging through his closet.

"When do you leave?" she asked him loudly. They had grown used to speaking with a wall between them.

"Tonight," he said. "Who knows for how long." He emerged from the closet holding two suits, but stopped halfway to the bed when he met Patricia's eyes. His looked more brown than hazel. Hers felt swollen and old.

"Are you all right?" he asked her.

"Well, to be honest..." Patricia began, but she couldn't finish the sentence. Even when she had accused her husband of an affair and she thought she hated him, she had told him exactly how she felt. She could do that with the man she loved: tell him the truth. But with strangers, and even certain friends, Patricia always strived to be good-natured instead of baldly honest.

"I want you to see Dr. Hartman," she told John, opting for simplicity instead of full disclosure. "I want you to go before you leave."

John frowned. "Pat... I don't know what's going on with you, but... don't you think the victims of an earthquake are more important—"

She held up her hand to stop him, glad for this easy out. "No, you're right. I was being selfish. Let's just get you packed."

Patricia picked up one of the suits he had selected and returned it to the closet. She exchanged it for a grey pinstriped one that fit him better, and turned to walk back into the room—but John was blocking her in.

"I have an idea," he said. "Why don't you call Dr. Hartman, ask if he could be flexible about the time and place we meet."

Instead of suggesting that they postpone the therapy until after he got back, instead of questioning her problems, John was being perfectly reasonable.

Like the ideal husband.

Patricia said, "I'll call Dr. Hartman tonight and find out if he's... flexible. Thank you... honey, for your understanding."

She handed the suit to him, then excused herself from the bedroom and disappeared into one of the guest rooms down the hallway. In the bathroom, Patricia sat on the toilet with the lid down, blowing cigarette smoke into the fan above her.

Flexible, she thought. Her "John" hadn't been flexible in years. She had always been an afterthought to her husband's ambitions. So had Scotty. Until he was dying. Then, finally, almost on his deathbed, their son got John's attention.

She took a long drag on her cigarette, then stared at the cloud of smoke floating toward the fan. Patricia had been hoping the cloud would turn black as some kind of sign that she was sleeping in the same bed with an imposter. But alas, the smoke was perfectly white.

She grabbed her phone to make the call to Dr. Hartman. If the doctor couldn't rearrange his schedule to speak with this imposter, then she would let that be her sign. By the time her "husband" came back from Syria, she would have all of her things moved out of the apartment, and she would have a divorce attorney on her side. The beautiful concept about hiring lawyers by the hour was that they always believed everything you told them. They had no reason to doubt a word you said as long as your checks cleared.

CHAPTER 23

THE MEDIA SWARMED RUTH GRANT'S house so quickly after her son had committed vehicular homicide on 151 people, it was as if his murderous act had shaken a hornet's nest.

More than a dozen satellite trucks, with logos from all the major networks and local news stations, lined the street. Everyone was shouting questions over the buzz of helicopters, which were shooting and sending aerial video to the press hives that would then distribute to the rest of the media world.

"What's a gangbang?" Carol Bryant asked. She posed her question as she sat in a triangle of folding chairs with a local news team—the on-air talent, Debbie Craig, and her cameraman, Dave.

The reporter frowned as she picked up her third slice. "What newspaper did you say you worked for?"

Before Carol could tell her again, the cameraman said, "I can't believe you've never heard of a gangbang."

They had been kind enough to invite Carol to share their dinner: takeout pizza from a local fast-food place. It was the "Aloha Special"—pineapple, coconut, and diced Spam, all atop three different cheeses with Hawaiian sweet bread as the crust.

Carol shrugged. "Hey, I just go where my assignment desk sends me."

Debbie said, "A gangbang, dear, is the same thing as a media orgy. Except only one person is getting screwed."

Carol looked embarrassed. "Oh. Well then, it truly is as vulgar as it sounds."

Dave burst out laughing.

"Glad to see my ignorance is your entertainment tonight," Carol said as she took a bite of her pizza.

The cameraman immediately stopped laughing and turned serious. "Nice perfume you're wearing."

Carol swallowed and used a napkin to wipe off the sloppy lipstick of sauce. "Thanks."

"Vanilla?" he guessed.

She nodded. "I'm going to have to stop wearing it before I eat myself to death."

Dave laughed at her joke. He was trying his best to be ingratiating, but his physical appearance mitigated his efforts. He sported long, shaggy hair as if he weren't north of fifty years old, and his faded and ripped windbreaker—embossed with the TV station logo—failed to cover the various food stains on his t-shirt, which was straining against his belly. Below the waist, he wore size forty-eight blue jeans, out of which his butt crack had been bursting for at least the last two years.

Debbie, the reporter, rolled her eyes at the two of them. She would have no problem regurgitating the pizza later if she spent two more minutes listening to them talk.

"So here's the question of the day," Dave said. "Why do you think he did it?"

"Who?" Carol asked.

Debbie said, "He's talking about Neal Grant, the killer. You have been taking notes in that pad of yours rather than just drawing smiley faces, right?"

"Oh," Carol said, "right. The accused killer." She didn't seem to take any offense to Debbie's sarcasm. "Yes, I definitely have a theory. But is it all right if you guys go first?"

Dave grinned, relishing the opportunity to give someone besides Debbie his point of view. "Well, my fearless reporter here is speculating that our killer lost his entire stock portfolio in the economic downturn. But my pet theory is way more of a personal nature, which, if I'm correct, triggers Debbie's theory as well. That's why I keep telling her that she's wrong, but not necessarily *wrong* wrong. I know I'm sounding sketchy, but I'm also hoping to sound intriguing at the same time. Please tell me you're still interested in what I have to say."

Carol dropped her pizza slice back into the box. "Please, I'm hanging on your every syllable."

Her response made Dave almost choke on the saliva that had been building in his mouth ever since he had met her.

"Well, thank you for your confidence. So here I go..." He leaned forward in his folding chair as if he had some juicy scandal to share with everyone. "I'm going all in and fingering Neal-what's-his-name's girlfriend. She's the missing link we don't know about yet, but we'll soon be told exists; she's the money ho who very recently dumped Neal's sorry ass and contacted a lawyer. Not necessarily in that order, I might point out.

"In fact, she's probably had this lawyer on retainer since she first met Neal while dancing in a Times Square strip joint, and she's told her legal representation all the things this Wall Street hotshot used to do to her behind closed bedroom doors... all of which surely was caught on tape. So now she and her ho-brother-in-arms legal aide decide to make these intimate shenanigans public, unless a certain someone makes several substantial payments for three years on the anniversary of the day these two love birds first met."

Dave finally sat back in his chair. "Well, there you go. That's my theory as to why we're all shivering our asses off in front of this house."

Before either of the female reporters could respond, Dave said, "Oh wait! One more thing—I want you both to notice I never said anything about how the mother of Neal-asshole-killing-machine is responsible for what her hell-inspired son did, because I don't believe she's responsible. I've done some things in my life that I never want my parents to know about, and I certainly don't want to put them in a situation where they have to stand in front of jerks like me as I frame them in my camera lens like they should be spit on by the rest of the viewing public...

"Okay," he said, "now I'm finished."

Carol stared at him as if he were a god. "That's amazing. I have to say, I'm totally turned on."

192

Hearing her reaction, Dave almost had a coronary right there on the spot. He tried to get out of his chair so he could bond with his new fan, but after a few unsuccessful attempts, he pretended as if he hadn't been trying at all.

"Thank you, Carol, for your support. Of course the final proof will be in the police press releases. If I'm right, we'll discover the killer's girlfriend-slash-scheming ho is one of the victims on the train."

Debbie had been listening slack-jawed to her dinner companions, but now she stood up and threw down her pizza slice, which had gone uneaten. She started to walk away, but couldn't resist and turned back around. "What did you say your name was?"

"Carol."

"Sorry, Carol, I got to ask... what was your theory?"

"Personally? I think Neal's violent act was a desperate attempt to anchor himself to some sort of reality—the reality of the flesh. Killing all of those innocent people... perhaps he thought it would prove he was still human. Dave here says the killer had one girlfriend, but I think in the days ahead we'll get evidence of a history of several one-night stands. When all of those empty hook-ups failed to fill the void, I'm guessing Neal realized he was digging a hole deeper and deeper until the only thing he could smell was his own sweat and desperation." She looked finished, but then she said, "Oh, wait! I also think he probably had an eating disorder. I just wish he and other people would realize the only thing separating us from the rest of the mammals is our dietary habits. Every human should probably cherish that."

Debbie nodded. "Well, thank you both for this surreal experience. It's been enlightening. Just let me know how much I owe for my share of the weed." She stormed off, only to stop a dozen feet away to pull out a hand mirror and check the gaps of her teeth for food.

After Debbie was out of earshot, Carol turned to the cameraman. "I think I hurt someone's feelings."

"Oh, forget about her," Dave said. "I really like your theory. In fact, I would love to discuss it with you further... How long does your desk expect you to hang around here? My shift ends at 8 a.m."

CHAPTER 24

RUTH GRANT FELT TRAPPED. Not only did she need a walker to get around the house, she couldn't stand at her own windows without ending up on the news in her nightgown and robe.

So she sat on the couch with the curtains drawn, staring at the dark screen of her old tube TV, which required a tuner box, it was so ancient.

She had turned it off because the news could only explain who, what, when and where, but not why. She couldn't explain it either, not even after hours of mulling over her last few interactions with her son.

Ruth's doorbell rang. The reporters had stopped ringing it when they found out she was practically a cripple. So maybe it was the police, back to tell her they had found her daughter.

Wincing and favoring her hip, Ruth climbed into her walker. "Who is it?" she called as she trundled toward the door.

"It's your nurse."

Confused, Ruth peeked out one of the narrow sidelights framing the door. The next nurse wasn't scheduled until nine, and the clock on the wall read a little after seven. Yet here a nurse was, standing on the stoop, surrounded by reporters.

Ruth let her in, and the nurse locked the door behind her, muffling the media's cries for attention.

"Mom," she said, stepping around the walker for a hug.

Ruth wheeled back, finally recognizing her daughter under the brown wig. "Why aren't you dead?"

Jenna winced.

"You called me," Ruth said. "You were in the car with him."

"Mom—"

"I checked the time, Jenna. On my phone. You called just minutes before the wreck."

"Mom, Neal, he—"

"He came here too, you know. With his face all cut up, and acting strange. And now you're here with bruises on your face. So I'll ask again, why aren't you—"

"Because I jumped!" Jenna cried, determined to get a word in edgewise. She hadn't meant to be so loud. Hopefully no one outside had heard her. "I jumped or I would be—"

"Come here," Ruth said, pulling her daughter close.

Jenna opened her arms, expecting a warm embrace, but Ruth wiped away her daughter's tears instead.

"I don't want anyone to see you crying, do you hear me?"

Jenna dried her eyes and suppressed the urge to glance out the side-light, deciding that she didn't want to be seen crying on national TV either. "Mom, did you say anything to the police? Anything about the fact that I was with Neal?"

"No," Ruth said. "I didn't want them finding another body." She knew how it sounded, but couldn't explain it any better. She had always struggled to rationalize what she considered to be the effeminate side of herself, so she typically ignored it. Because expressing it was infinitively more difficult.

"What about your nurse?" Jenna said. "Your real nurse. Is she here?"

"She called in sick," Ruth said. "Probably didn't want to be seen on TV, working for the mother of a mass murderer."

Jenna nodded. "Come on then. We need to go back to your bedroom." She reached out to help her mother along.

"Why?" Ruth asked.

"Because I need to talk to you. Away from all these windows."

"Fine. I guess it's my naptime anyway." Ruth started to wheel herself down the hallway to her bedroom, ignoring Jenna's offer to help even though it was obvious she needed more support to bear all the weight. Jenna's mother always had a way of making it seem as if Jenna were treating her like a child.

Ruth's intention, which Jenna would never know, was to leave strong footsteps for her children to follow. She didn't want help. Anyone who needed it left themselves vulnerable. That was the example she had spent her entire life trying to set.

Except Ruth had forgotten one important thing: she usually relied on a nurse to get her into bed.

"At least let me help you with that," Jenna said, watching her mother try to swing her legs onto the mattress.

Ruth, almost sweating from the pain, finally nodded. The nurse uniform fit Jenna so well. And that's what she was: just another nurse. If Ruth could convince herself of that, then she could get through the indignity.

Jenna lifted her feet and got her turned around.

"Prop me up," Ruth said. "On those pillows. And be a dear and fetch me my pills."

Jenna did everything her mother asked, but kept an eye on the clock. George had said they didn't have long.

Once Ruth felt clearheaded and settled, she said, "Why?"

"Huh?" Jenna asked, straightening the duvet.

"I just... I want to know why."

"Why what, Mom?"

"Why he did it."

Jenna glanced at her, and then smoothed out the last edge of the comforter. She decided to take her mother's cue and speak without emotion. "He was trying to kill me, Mom."

Ruth responded instantly, so Jenna knew her mother had probably been processing it for hours before she showed up.

"No, I don't believe that. Neal loved you. I can think of, in fact I've already been thinking of, dozens and dozens of times when he did the exact opposite of what you're implying. I thought you were always the really smart one of the two, but that answer is just plain dumb. Maybe we should check under your wig for any more bruises across your skull."

Jenna sighed and sat on the edge of the mattress. She needed to tell her mother everything that had happened, but she didn't think she could. Not because of the grief, but because of her exhaustion, and the time it would take to explain.

She took a deep breath and resolved to get it over with. In one long sentence, she told Ruth everything up to the moment when Neal drove his car into the train, skipping the part about the strangler in the field. She still hadn't come up with any explanation for the man's actions, and she knew her mother would only worry... and berate her for not solving that particular mystery yet.

Jenna also left out the part about George. She was still questioning her choice to let him call the shots. The last thing she needed was to endure her mother's take on that situation as well.

Ruth listened impassively to her daughter's story, wincing only when she shifted her weight to favor her hip. Once her daughter was done, she said, "It must have been his bike accident. Maybe a head injury or... Neal just would never do anything like this."

"That's what I thought," Jenna said. "But he seemed pretty normal to me. Not really himself, but certainly not... dangerous. How could an injury make him selectively homicidal like that, and not outright crazy?"

Under her breath, Ruth said, "I didn't know you borrowed his money for a doctorate in psychology as well..."

Jenna folded her hands in her lap and stared down at them. She hated when she presumed expertise in other sciences. And she hated when her mother made a point at her expense.

"He came to visit me," Ruth said, staring off into space. "Last weekend."

She took so long to continue that Jenna was preparing to leave.

"I knew it wasn't him because he had quit snapping back," Ruth said.

"Snapping back? I don't—"

"You know how we used to fight? Little things, like how I didn't want him buying me a new coffee pot, or how many paper towels the nurses were using?"

"Yeah," Jenna said. Their bickering had always made holidays and family gatherings loads of fun.

"I always taught you kids to be fighters. But Neal, after the accident... I'd never seen him so ingratiating." She chuckled to herself. "I thought at first maybe I'd worn him down."

They shared a moment of silence because they both knew just how wrong she had been.

"That's how I knew you were still you," Ruth said, meeting Jenna's eyes. "Because you yelled at me."

The edge of the mattress had become increasingly uncomfortable. Jenna stood and started to leave. "See if you can get some rest, Mom."

"Where are you going?"

"Just into the next room. I'll be right back." She wanted to see what other mess Neal might have left behind.

———

JENNA SEARCHED THE KITCHEN first but found nothing, so she moved to her mother's den. Neal had always called it her man cave. Bones and artifacts cluttered the bookcases and sill; green leather upholstered the chairs.

The wig was itching her, so Jenna took it off and set it aside. She sat down at her mother's desk and sorted through a pile of papers on the blotter. Just pages of correspondence between Ruth and her old colleagues, letters written in longhand ink. Jenna smiled. Her mother was probably the last person on earth who still mailed and received letters sealed with wax.

In the desk drawer, Jenna found stacks of bills and her mother's checkbook. In the last two months, all of the checks had been written by Neal.

She skimmed a few of the bills and found one from an auto-mechanic dated last week for work done on Neal's BMW. The receipt said, "Accidental airbag deployment. Bags somehow damaged. Replacements on order."

Jenna covered her mouth.

Had her brother planned all of this? Her death. His?

She nearly screamed when she heard a footstep outside.

Wooden blinds obscured the window directly behind her. She couldn't see anything through it, but she knew it overlooked the back yard. Hedges rustled right on the other side of the glass.

With a trembling hand, Jenna reached for the blinds. At the last second, she pulled back.

My wig! she thought. She had almost exposed herself to whoever was out there. Jenna put the brown hair back on and sat for a second, listening. She didn't hear any more noises from outside.

Slowly, carefully, she lifted one of the slats in the blinds. A man was staring back at her. His camera hovered inches from the glass.

"Hey!" Jenna shouted. She threw aside the shutters and thrust open the window, ready to yell some pretty nasty things.

The cameraman, just some clown in blue jeans and a windbreaker, fell backward out of the hedges and stared at her in mortal terror for a few seconds. Then he scrambled back over the privacy fence, losing a shoe in the process.

Jenna marched outside and snatched up the man's sneaker before he got a chance to come back for it. It was going straight into her mother's trash.

Thank God I remembered the wig, Jenna thought. Then she thought a moment longer, about the fact that she had originally... thanked God. That was when Jenna realized from there on out, nothing would ever be the same.

———

AFTER GOING THROUGH SOME OLD BOXES of notes and essays from college, Jenna returned to the master bedroom, where her mother was still sitting up in bed, wide awake.

"Did you find anything?" Ruth asked, noticing the file of papers in Jenna's hand.

"No, not really." Jenna had hidden her brother's automotive bill in her pocket. "Like you said, he probably had a brain injury. Hospital just didn't catch it."

Ruth nodded, and for the first time that night, Jenna saw her face relax; her mother looked so much older than she remembered.

"He just would never intentionally hurt all those people," Ruth said. "Not the Neal I raised."

Jenna sat down next to her and took her hand, which felt more like skin and bones than flesh and blood. Her mother had gotten so skinny.

"Are you going to be all right?" Jenna asked.

Ruth nodded. "You know what I've always told you kids."

"What, the key to life?"

"Yep. You just have to stand up and take it."

"But, Mom, you just had hip surgery."

"Well then... that's no excuse. I'll just have to lie down and take it."

Jenna smiled. Her mother always had been horrible at jokes, even in her lecture series. "Listen, Mom... I have to leave for a while. I'll call you tonight, okay?"

She stood up, but Ruth held onto her hand.

"Where are you going?"

"I want to check in with the people Neal worked with. They probably have a lot of questions."

Ruth nodded. "I wish you were staying."

Jenna knew her mother well enough to understand what she meant. Protecting her daughter was an instinct that would never go away, even as she had no choice but to let her daughter go.

———

DAVE, THE CAMERAMAN, came limping back to the news van, missing a shoe. The reporter, Debbie, smiled at him from her folding chair. "What happened to you?"

"Don't ask," he said. He sat down and motioned toward Carol's chair, which was empty. "Where'd she go?"

Debbie shrugged. "Don't ask me. I'm not the one putting the moves on her."

The cameraman looked around the crowd. "That's weird. She ran off when the nurse got here, but I thought she'd be coming back. You'd think she'd want a quote."

"Yeah, well maybe a real reporter would want an interview with the nurse, but I keep telling you she isn't a real reporter," Debbie said. She opened the pizza box, but all that was left were the chunks of meat Carol had picked off her slices.

CHAPTER 25

ARKED AT THE CURB two blocks from the media circus, George waited in his little blue car, researching Dr. Fincher on Jenna's smartphone. He focused especially on Fincher's new relationship with Envoy John Wolfenson, who, apparently, the President was sending to Syria for earthquake relief. George had no doubt Fincher would tag along.

He was navigating to a travel site to find plane tickets out of D.C. when Jenna's phone signaled an incoming text. The sender was someone by the name of Raymond Chappell.

George checked the rearview mirror to see if Jenna was coming. She wasn't. He opened the message.

It read, *Why'd you ask about that French Ambassador? Heard on the news he was killed!*

George read the text several times. He couldn't figure out why she might have mentioned Tottone to anyone. He explored deeper into her records, and within a few screen taps he discovered an entire conversation between her and Raymond, part of it involving the Codex Gigas. She had drilled him for information. It begged the question, did she know enough to translate the pages?

Another incoming text pinged Jenna's inbox. *Please let me know you're all right*, Raymond had written.

George took his time absorbing this message too. *Her boyfriend?* he wondered. Definitely someone who cared about her.

In the rearview, camera flashes caught his attention. Jenna, swarmed by cameramen and reporters, was approaching the car, head down.

Quickly, George fired up the engine and leaned over the passenger seat to throw open her door.

"Can you tell us if Mrs. Grant said anything to you about her son?" one of the reporters shouted as Jenna climbed in.

"Did you ever meet Neal Grant?" another woman asked.

Jenna slammed the door in their faces and slapped a file folder down onto her lap. Her notes to crack the Codex code, George assumed.

"Go," she said, and he inched his way through the reporters.

Jenna looked back at her mother's house.

"She'll be all right," George said once they were a safe distance from all the eyes and ears. "No one will harm her—not with a camera looking in every window."

"I know," Jenna said. She threw her wig into the back seat, onto the leather portfolio containing the Codex Gigas pages and the notebook of translations. George had decided against leaving the documents in his apartment. Too vulnerable there. Not that carrying them around wasn't dangerous.

"What now?" Jenna asked.

"I don't know. That's what I need to figure out. Have you translated all of the pages?"

"The ones that count. It's pretty rough, though. And I still need to translate that last page."

"Think you can do it?"

"With these notes? Yeah."

"Think Raymond could help?"

Jenna stared at him. "How'd you know about Raymond?"

George shrugged. "You searched my house. I read your texts."

"He texted me?" Jenna grabbed her phone and checked her messages.

George watched her read them. She pored through each one, and then hurried to the next.

"Who is he?" George asked.

"My radio show co-host. In London."

"So he could help us then."

"Do you mean with the pages?"

"Yes."

Jenna grimaced. "I don't want this to come off the wrong way, but... he's not as smart as I am."

George raised an eyebrow.

"Don't get me wrong, Raymond is extremely clever. And his father was an Anglican minister, so he's probably better suited for this type of situation, but—to be honest, we don't need to involve him in this."

"Okay," George said.

"I'm going to text him, tell him I'm all right."

George nodded and looked around at the passing scenery while she typed. They were moving through the small town of Occoquan, down Mill Street. Shops and restaurants flanked both sides, and through the alleys, George caught flashes of the Occoquan River.

"So," he said once Jenna had sent her text, "this is where you grew up?"

"Yep. Hasn't changed a bit. But I guess that's the point."

Occoquan, as a tourist destination, evoked the era of the Civil War, both in décor and architecture. Historically, it had served as the main post office between the North and the South. Confederate forces had actually headquartered there.

"So what does an evolutionary psychologist make of a town that hasn't evolved since before abolition?" Jenna asked George.

He glanced at her, surprised by the remark. He didn't remember mentioning his occupation to her. But even if he had told her, it impressed him how she incorporated the information into her observations.

"Well, someone making a snap judgment might conclude that our surroundings are indeed in evolutionary stasis. But I would point out that the town has survived decades precisely because it has... *evolved.* It's become a tourist community. I would call your hometown a perfect example of economic Darwinism in action."

"Interesting," Jenna said. "In high school we all just thought we lived in a tourist trap. George, you've just given me a whole different way to look at this place."

More than that, his answer had relieved her. It was good to know he was still in touch with the man he used to be, before the train wreck.

But even Neal had remembered Jenna's lifelong dream to stay in The Willard, so maybe George had retained his memories too.

She needed to perform one final test.

"Do you mind?" Jenna asked, reaching for the power-window button on her door panel. "I'm a little warm..."

George's eyes flicked between her and the road, and his hands tightened on the steering wheel.

Jenna pressed the button, and her window started to roll down.

"Please," George said, tensing up as if he were driving through a snowstorm. "I'll turn on the air conditioner. Just—please... roll up your window."

Jenna hated herself. She knew Carri had fallen out of this very window, and she knew how George might react. But she had needed to see if he would. And he had.

He had passed the test.

She hit the button on the armrest to roll up the window. But the glass failed to slide up. The little motor just buzzed and buzzed. Jenna apologized and punched the button a couple of times.

"Whoa—hold on!" George cried, throwing his arm across her chest as he slammed on the brakes.

A woman was walking in the middle of the street.

The car's tires screeched on the pavement, and the car stopped a few feet from the woman, who simply kept walking, twisting her head around to stare at Jenna, even as she disappeared down one of the driver's-side alleys.

"Oh my God—that's her!" Jenna said. "That's the blonde!" She threw open her door to get out.

"Don't!" George said. "It's a trap!"

Jenna slammed the door behind her.

As she marched across the road toward the alley, she glanced up and down the street. It was late in the evening, and the shops had closed. At the end of the strip, a few people were smoking cigarettes outside a restaurant, but that was it.

George quickly nosed into one of the diagonal parking spaces that lined the one-way road. He was getting out of the car when a bolt of pain shot through him.

He reached for the door handle, but missed and collapsed in his seat, gasping. For the last couple of hours, he had been dismissing the pangs in his chest. Now his ribs felt so cracked he could barely breathe.

He watched helplessly as Jenna disappeared into the darkness between buildings.

Behind the main street, she emerged into a courtyard serving five stores, only one of which cast light: a New Age shop called The Ninth Planet. Some of Jenna's high school friends had worked there every summer. The motto on the sign, which the owner, Kelli Langton, had painted, read, "Celebrating Pluto, Sunshine, and the Spirit Within."

Kelli's front door stood wide open.

Jenna crept to the center of the courtyard, but then froze as cloaked figures stepped out of hiding all around her. Some of them leapt and lunged, and then flickered back, just tricks of the light, cast by the candles lighting up Kelli's shop.

Jenna let out a quivering breath and strode over to the open door. She took a tentative step inside, leaning this way and that to peek around display tables and racks.

She had imagined just a few candles, not hundreds of them, were providing the light. But every single stick of wax on every single shelf and tabletop burned. The various hot waxes reeked of sage, rosemary, and myrrh.

The only part of the shop not illuminated was the front counter area, behind the cash register. Someone stood back there in the dark, back in the shadow cast by a partial wall. It was Kelli, Jenna knew; she recognized the silhouette of the shop owner's frizzy hair.

"Mrs. Langton—hi! Listen, I think someone came in here..." As Jenna made her way around a few tables of oils, tarot cards, and Merkabah figurines, she noticed Kelli wasn't responding. The storeowner just stood there, slanted to one side in the dark, perfectly still. And smiling, from the looks of it.

"Kelli?"

The front door of the shop slammed shut. A cold, powerful gust swept through, brightening the flames seconds before snuffing them out. And in that one bright moment before the blackout, Kelli Langton's body lit up with candles at her feet. Hundreds of wax sticks had been melted into a sort of altar up to her waist: a miniature Gothic cathedral of black paraffin spires tipped in finial flames.

The burst of light was so bright and so brief, it burnt an image into Jenna's eyes. She could still see it, even after the cold gust had left the room completely dark. She could still see Kelli Langton's corpse: illuminated, stiffened with instant rigor mortis from her violent, strenuous death and then propped up against the herb wall along the back of the shop.

Kelli's throat smiled wetly ear to ear.

Jenna stood absolutely frozen for several heartbeats, clamping a hand over her mouth, holding her breath, holding a scream, her face red from the pressure.

When they were little, she and her brother had joked that Kelli was a witch, evidenced by her frizzy white hair and the crystal balls featured prominently in her store. Now Kelli was dead, killed by something much more of a witch than she had ever been.

Jenna decided to run.

She crashed into one of the tables, heard glass shattering, heard metal clatter on wood. She stumbled, tripped. She held her hands out in front of her and fumbled along the table of Merkabah figurines, back toward the entrance.

"Sis!" Neal cried out, as if his voice were coming from the sound system of the shop. "Sis, please!"

In the farthest reaches of the store, a few candles flared to life. One of them spotlighted Neal's face, which was free of scabs, but stricken with terror. "They've got me!"

Someone's shadow moved in front of him, eclipsed him, and the few candles went out, leaving the shop dark again.

"Sis!"

In the darkness, Jenna heard herself whimpering, weeping, as if the sounds were coming from someone else. She wanted to call out her brother's name. Wanted to run to him, help him. But he was an illusion. Had to be.

Neal was dead.

She turned to keep going, but a rack of votives in front of her exploded with fire. Jenna jumped back and screamed.

The blonde from the motel stepped in front of the exit. She reeked of vanilla and pizza and shit, and her face had been stretched, as if from too much plastic surgery. A thick, white film covered her pupils, which were completely dilated and pale blue, like two cobalt pearls floating in coconut milk.

"The Codex pages," she said, her voice raspy and distant. "Give them to us."

"I don't have them!" Jenna said, backing up.

"Then your brother pays."

In the far corner of the shop, another set of candles burst into brightness. This time, Neal's face began to hemorrhage and bleed. "Jenna—help! Help!"

The candles fizzled out, but he kept shrieking in pain.

"That's not my brother," Jenna said. "That's not him."

"It is. His soul belongs to us now. And he will burn and suffer and suppurate pus until you give us what we want."

Without another word, the blonde leapt forward and clamped a purple-veined claw around Jenna's throat. "Where are the pages? Tell us, or join your brother in hell!"

Jenna flailed helplessly as her lungs began to burn and the world began to dim.

"Last chance," the blonde said. Her grip eased up so Jenna could speak. "Where are the pages?"

"Not here," Jenna said, gurgling, gasping.

Before she could say anything more, the shop's front window exploded inward. George, shedding glass, landed on both feet just behind the blonde.

He reached for Jenna, but a crystal ball shot toward him like a bullet. He ducked, and the orb smashed into the wall.

The blonde released Jenna's throat and dragged her by the hair toward the back of the store.

George tried to follow, but the shelf of crystal balls began to vibrate. One by one, they shot toward George. He ducked and dodged the first two, but the third one punched him in the gut. George collapsed to his knees, breathless.

The blonde laughed at him, a horrible, guttural sound, more animal than human.

Jenna, sitting now as she was dragged along, kicked her feet and clawed at the blonde's hand. She slipped around in a pool of Kelli Langton's blood, which had grown sticky and cold. Her left foot hit one of the shelves, and a box of magic wands spilled onto the ground. She grabbed for one, but the blonde stomped it, snapped it, and kicked it away. Then she pulled Jenna through a beaded curtain into the back room.

"I'm only going to ask you this one more time!" the blonde screamed as she pinned Jenna to the floor. "Where are the—" She stopped mid-sentence, sensing or hearing something behind her. By the time she turned around, it was too late to defend herself.

George barreled through the beaded curtain and shoved the broken magic wand, purple and dipped in sparkles, deep into the blonde's left eye. Blood spattered on Jenna's face a few seconds before the blonde crumpled on top of her, lifeless, still. Jenna pushed her off.

During the confrontation, the buttons on George's shirt had broken off and he was pretty much exposed from the waist up.

He fell to his knees.

"Are you okay?" Jenna asked, hurrying to his side.

He didn't answer her.

"Oh my God, George!" She had caught sight of several large bruises covering his chest. "Is that from the crystal balls?"

He looked down and seemed almost as stunned at the sight as she was. George climbed to his feet, trying his best to shake it off. "Come on," he said, breathless and strained. He started back toward the exit. Jenna followed with a hand on his back, supporting him.

"Wait," she said before they went out the front door. She turned on the lights and looked around. She didn't see her brother. Didn't expect to.

Jenna shut off the fluorescents and let Kelli Langton rest in peace.

CHAPTER 26

PATRICIA AND JOHN WOLFENSON shared the back seat of the limousine, but there couldn't have been more space between them. Dr. Hartman noticed it immediately when he climbed into the opposite seat.

"Good evening, doctor," Wolfenson said.

"Good *late* evening," Hartman replied. "Well past my bedtime."

Patricia was the only one too nervous to react to the joke.

"I saw your skit the other night," Hartman told Wolfenson as the chauffer pulled away from the curb, headed for the Dulles International Airport. "Absolutely hilarious."

"Oh, thank you. Watching me bungle lines was probably very entertaining."

The skit, part of a late-night comedy program, had focused on a husband and wife who did nothing but argue. The couple had decided to bring on the best marriage counselor imaginable: the man who had brought peace to the Middle East, John Wolfenson. Of course, not even a diplomat could settle the couple's latest spat.

"Well, bungled lines or not, the audience absolutely loved you," Hartman said with a grin.

When he had met Wolfenson years ago, Hartman had enjoyed the politician's company. That much hadn't changed. And the envoy certainly appeared to be the same man, save for the three-inch scar running from his left ear to the base of his neck. Wolfenson's eyes did seem more brown than hazel, and he did look thinner, healthier. But as his wife had pointed out, he had forsaken alcohol, processed foods, and red meat; a healthy glow was to be expected.

The limousine had turned onto Constitution Avenue, and Patricia gazed out the window, suppressing a sigh. Her therapist wasn't treating the situation with the gravity it merited.

She needed a cigarette.

"So, John," Hartman said, sensing Patricia's aggravation. "Have you noticed anything different about yourself since... that day?"

"Are we referring to the peace accord, or the attack?" Wolfenson asked.

Hartman realized how awkwardly he had transitioned into the topic. "I'm sure that both events affected you deeply. I imagine in different ways, so... both."

Now it was Wolfenson's turn to look out the window, out across the Ellipse to the White House, lit up amongst the trees, as if it generated its own divine light. He seemed to be focusing on something beyond the mansion, some distant memory. "I suppose by itself, the peace accord would have been profoundly fulfilling. But the attack that day, and what happened afterward... it changed me in an equally profound way."

"Maybe it would help if you gave me some examples."

"Sure. Let's see... I guess I'm more focused on what I do every day. Focused on accomplishing more with my life." He lifted Patricia's hand and kissed it. "I'm also focused on enjoying the person I love, and who loves me."

Patricia held his hand, though it felt different, warmer, stranger, and very uncomfortable. The John she knew had rarely shown her physical affection in public. She hoped that Dr. Hartman remembered that detail from couples therapy.

"What happened after the attack that caused this... focus?"

"To be accurate," Wolfenson said, "it's what didn't happen."

"Sorry. I'm not sure I follow."

"Well... we've all heard of near-death experiences: the light at the end of the tunnel; people seeing their loved ones who've passed away. I was technically dead for several minutes, but... I didn't see any of that." Wolfenson once again raised his wife's hand to his lips and kissed it. "Not even our son."

Again, Patricia looked out the window, this time trying her best not to cry. Twilight lingered in the Potomac River far below the Teddy Roosevelt Bridge, though the world had long since fallen into the dark.

"All I saw when I died was black," Wolfenson said, looking directly at Hartman. "A complete and utter void."

"And how would that change you?" Dr. Hartman asked.

Patricia, composed now, turned to gauge the sincerity of Wolfenson's response, and to find any hidden meaning behind it.

The envoy spoke with even more intensity and passion. "No matter what life I have here, that's all there is. There's no life after death. At least not for me. So I better make the best of it."

Dr. Hartman nodded. "Well, you are definitely a changed man. I can see that for myself. And I can also see why someone close to you might even think you're not the same man at all."

Hartman had tried to phrase it as a general statement, to cleverly introduce the idea without violating Patricia's privacy. He hadn't taken into account just how bright the envoy could be.

"Is that what this is about?" Wolfenson asked his wife. "You think I'm... different?"

Hartman tried to change the subject. "John, if it's okay with you, I'd like to—"

"No," Patricia said, staring Wolfenson down. "Not just different. You're an imposter."

Wolfenson practically flinched. And, surprisingly, Patricia believed his reaction. She had confused him. Dr. Hartman believed that she had even hurt him.

For several seconds, the hum of the limo's engine and wheels was the only sound. Wolfenson opened his mouth a few times only to shut it. He looked over at the therapist, who offered only a neutral expression. Patricia began to cry.

Finally, Wolfenson grabbed Patricia's hands. "I may be different than I was a few months ago, but I am still your husband. I am the exact same man who first asked you out while wearing a dress."

Dr. Hartman was glad to see Patricia reflexively giggle. He knew the story of how the Wolfensons had met. For theatre arts in college, John once had played a role in which the male character disguised himself as a woman. Patricia, backstage to meet a girlfriend who was also in the play, had run into John in full costume.

"I'm also the same jerk who didn't call you for two weeks after the first time we slept together. And the father who held our son's hand when he was dying in the hospital."

Patricia looked away, biting her lip.

"Patricia, please, look at me. It's me, John." Tears rolled down Wolfenson's cheeks. Patricia didn't want to believe in them, didn't want to accept them as anything more than crocodile tears.

Wolfenson wiped them away. Suddenly, he sat forward and tapped the privacy partition separating the back seat from the chauffer. "Take us back home," the envoy said as the glass divider rolled down.

Patricia took hold of his arm. "John, what are you doing?"

"Canceling the trip."

"No," Patricia said. "People are dying. They need you."

"I don't care. This is my marriage and it's the most important thing to me."

Patricia turned to Dr. Hartman. "Please, tell him to go. Tell him that I'll be fine."

Before Hartman could respond, Wolfenson said, "What if you came with me?"

Patricia and Dr. Hartman exchanged a glance.

"I know it's not like going on a honeymoon," Wolfenson said, "but we'll be together."

"No, I can't," Patricia said. "I didn't bring anything. No clothes, no..."

He pulled her closer. "Whatever you need, we'll buy in Tel Aviv. I just, I want to be with you. I want to convince you—*reconnect* with you. I'm begging you, give me this chance."

"I don't know..." Patricia said.

She knew if she went, she would be stuck with someone she didn't trust in a devastated area where someone could easily disappear. But if she didn't go, she feared he would cancel the trip, and more people would die because of it. And maybe she would lose the only man she had ever loved.

"Sir," the chauffer said, "shall I continue to the airport?"

No one had the answer.

CHAPTER 27

"WE NEED TO GO TO THE POLICE," Jenna said as she drove out of Occoquan. George had let her drive because he didn't want to be the one behind the wheel when the pains in his chest returned.

"You don't understand," he said. "What we're up against... this goes much higher than the police."

"Yeah, but Mrs. Langton... I can't just—" Jenna wiped at a bloodstain on her cheek, wiped at her tears. "We need to at least leave an anonymous tip."

"I get it," George said. "Believe me, I do. But if you call the cops, even anonymously, they'll look at the security cameras. They'll find us, and they'll question us, and in the meantime a lot more people will die."

"Well," Jenna said, scrambling for some kind of compromise. "At least let me take you to the hospital, get you checked out."

"No," George said. "Hospitals are the first place cops put out their feelers. No."

Jenna shook her head. The only time she had seen someone as pale as George was when she was twelve years old, working on her mother's dig in Iraq with one of Ruth's colleagues. The portly anthropologist had practically bled sweat in the sun. Like George, the man had sounded as if he were breathing with a collapsed lung. By the time Jenna had fetched her mother, the anthropologist had keeled over. She would never forget his eyes, almost black from the dilated pupils. George's eyes were just as black.

"So what's your plan then?" she asked.

"Our clothes. We need new ones."

Jenna agreed. Kelli Langton's blood, and fluids from the blonde's eye, had stained the nurse's outfit. The fabric practically crawled across her skin. "We could go to a Wal-Mart, or..."

"Okay," George said. "I'll go in."

Jenna didn't think he looked up to walking, but she acquiesced. She certainly couldn't go into public looking like she had just murdered someone.

"Tell me something," she said. "What exactly did you kill back there?"

George took a few moments to formulate a response. He felt that any answer could push her over the edge.

"Because I'm not sure it was human," Jenna added.

"No, she was human. Just... possessed."

"Possessed? By what? Satan?"

"No, probably not Satan," George said. "One of his demons."

"Demons," Jenna said, under her breath.

"Yes, that's right. Demons."

"Okay, so how do you know all of this, George? Wait... a better question is—did you know any of it before the train crash?"

He thought a long time before responding. "I don't know. That's a good question. Because of my work, I've had plenty of connections with religion and the concepts that go with the territory. And my field certainly debates the concept of religious belief and whether, after thousands of years, it has become a dominant feature in our genetic code. But I can't recall ever doing very much research into demons and human possession."

Jenna kept on driving. George could tell she had something on her mind, but he let her take her time sorting it all out.

"My brother," she finally said. "Was he possessed?"

"Yes," George replied. If Jenna was looking for something more beyond his quick response, she chose not to ask for clarification, deciding instead to drive the rest of the way to the store in silence.

———

GEORGE GRABBED A SPARE COAT that he kept in his trunk just in case his car ever broke down in freezing weather. He put it on and buttoned it up to cover his torn-open shirt and the horrible bruises beneath.

In the department store, he moved up and down the aisles, tossing shirts, blouses, pants, coats, gloves, shoes, and anything else that looked like something they might wear in the next few days. The funny thing was that his cart looked no different than the carts of other customers waiting in line to pay.

A few miles up the road from the store, George directed Jenna to pull into a gas station, and they both went into the little bathroom to try on their new clothes.

While she dressed in the stall, George changed in front of one of the mirrors. He left his shirt unbuttoned so he could examine the black and purple bruises covering his chest. His abdomen was starting to discolor as well.

George dampened a paper towel with cold water from the sink and wiped the sweat from his face.

He heard Jenna preparing to exit the stall, and he quickly buttoned his shirt.

She stepped out in a new pair of jeans and a white blouse. "So how do I look?" she asked. "Like my brother just tried to kill me?"

George sighed. She probably meant to be humorous, but her voice had trembled.

Ever since the train accident, George had been astounded by Jenna's will to move forward. For him, coming to terms with the wreck had been easy; in a weird way, it wasn't even a choice. Something had happened to him during the crash. He still wasn't quite sure what. Someone he loved had appeared to him. But for Jenna, someone she loved had tried to kill her. Up to this point she had somehow stood strong.

It was her strength that pushed George to compare her to Carri. His wife had been the toughest person he had ever met. Once, she had shaved her head in moral support to help her teenage niece through chemotherapy. Another time, she had stepped between a charging pit bull and a smaller dog that she had been walking for a neighbor.

Scratched and bitten, Carri had needed stitches, but she never once complained.

"Where to now?" Jenna asked.

George met her eyes in the bathroom mirror. "I want you to take me to the airport. Before I get on the plane, you're going to tell me everything you know about the Codex Gigas pages. And then—" He coughed.

For a moment, Jenna thought he would hack up blood, but he cleared his throat and was fine.

"And then," he said, "that will be the end for you."

Jenna frowned, shook her head. "Why? Because of the joke about my brother? I'm not even sure why I said it. I'm fine. As they say in my trade, 'Give me a shovel and tell me which hole I'm digging in today.'"

George took a step toward her. "Believe me, I know you think you're fine. But you're not. When someone close to you dies, you go into a fog. Now, I know you've been very sharp since this ordeal began. But the fog's coming. Perhaps it's already here. You're going to start asking yourself all sorts of... introspective questions. Questions that you absolutely should ask. But for me, those questions will only get in the way of what I have to do... what I was brought back from the dead to do."

Jenna's eyes drifted down to his chest. Sweat had already dampened his light-blue sports shirt, had made the thin, cheap fabric transparent. She could see the bruises, the extent of them.

"Look at yourself," she said, and George shifted his eyes to the mirror. "Whatever you need to do, you won't be able to do it alone."

She leaned into George so that her reflection appeared beside his. "You're right I have questions that I want to have answered. Starting with—I need to know why my brother did this. And I want to meet the person or... whatever was responsible. But there's no *fog*. You show me the fog."

George noticed there was no longer a tremble in her voice. And in the mirror, he could see her eyes had refocused. Perhaps she was stronger than he had imagined.

"If you were brought back from the dead for a reason," she said, "then so was I."

"I can see why you feel that way, but—"

"How are you going to get the pages through customs, George, have you thought about that?"

He had to admit that he hadn't.

"Now I, on the other hand, move artifacts all the time. I know some of these guys in customs by name. One I even dated."

George tried to think of a valid counterpoint, but couldn't. "Fine," he said, "okay. But we'll need your passport."

Jenna said, "Then I guess we're going back to the hotel..."

———

AT THE WILLARD, George left Jenna in the car. He made his way to the concierge desk, where a woman greeted him almost as if they had met before.

"Here to pick up the young lady's things?" she asked.

"So you spoke with her," George said.

"Yes, a few minutes ago."

228

He nodded. He had known the answer already.

On the drive to the hotel, he had instructed Jenna to call ahead that a friend would be claiming her belongings; she couldn't come herself because her brother had recently caused a major train accident. At first, Jenna couldn't believe he wanted to proceed that way, but George convinced her it would be easier. Her involvement in the ordeal would sweep aside any hotel policies about releasing personal belongings to anyone but the owner, as long as Jenna could prove her identity over the phone by reciting her driver's license and describing the contents of her purse, which she had done.

"What a tragedy," the concierge said. "I hope she's okay."

George decided to say nothing, that it would be better if he simply looked grim. The woman gave him Jenna's purse and carry-on bag, and told him to take care.

On his way out, George stopped at a trashcan. He could hear piano music coming from the bar, the song "As Time Goes By" from *Casablanca*, one of Carri's favorite films. She considered it a "relationship test" movie. If she was serious about a guy, she would make him watch it. If he didn't like it, she would stop dating him. George hadn't known about the test, and the first time he watched the movie he had fallen asleep. Carri disregarded the test result and tried again a month later. George, still clueless, fell asleep again. She ended up marrying him anyway.

Standing over the trashcan, George opened Jenna's purse and pulled out her passport. In her photograph, she smiled impishly, exactly like the image of her George had seen in his mind's eye directly after the train wreck. It didn't surprise him.

He held the document over the trashcan. Acquiring a new passport would take Jenna weeks. She would be stuck in the States, completely unable to follow George overseas, an ocean and a continent away. It would save her life.

But he didn't drop it. And not just because he needed her help transporting the pages. For some reason, she was important.

George hoped to hear his wife's voice, offering guidance, but he heard only the song, "As Time Goes By."

CHAPTER 28

THE DULLES INTERNATIONAL AIRPORT, in operation since 1962, sat amidst farmland. The terminal building, with its swooping roof and floor-to-ceiling windows, symbolized flight.

George bought two tickets to Tel Aviv. Luckily, for the first leg of their journey, he managed to book two seats together in business class.

"Where's the layover?" Jenna asked.

"London. Why?"

"No reason."

On the plane, George asked for a pillow and a blanket and shortly fell asleep. Combined with the thrum of the engines, his loud, steady breathing created a pocket of white noise, like Jenna's own private study. It allowed her to fully concentrate on the eighth and final page of the Codex Gigas, copied into her notebook. The files she had retrieved from her mother's house contained translations of the Bingen code, which she used to decipher the cryptic exorcism.

After a few hours of painstaking work, and a few beers from the beverage cart, she looked around the cabin for anyone who might have been watching her. It was a red-eye flight, so most of the passengers had fallen asleep, and the ones who *were* awake seemed to be caught up in the e-books they were reading or the work they were doing on their laptops.

Jenna looked over at George, still fast asleep.

"Oh my God," she muttered to herself.

George's pillow, once white, was now soaked with blood.

She gently shook him awake. "Look," she said, pointing.

George blushed and quickly hid the pillow under his blanket. He looked around to see if anyone had seen. Jenna gave him some Kleenex from her purse, and he wiped his nose.

"Has the bleeding stopped?" he whispered.

She nodded, and then rested her hand over his. "It's all right. Nobody saw."

He took a heavy breath and stared down at the shape of the pillow beneath the blanket. "You know I have dreams when I sleep."

Jenna didn't know how to respond.

He looked up at her, and his pupils, still fully dilated, glowed in the soft yellow light. "That means I'm alive, right?"

"What?" Jenna asked, practically shouting it, she was so startled by his question. People glanced over, and she dropped back to a whisper. "Why on earth would you think you're not alive?"

"Because I shouldn't be. And because I saw Carri on the train, her ghost. I figured maybe that's what I am... like her."

"That's ridiculous, George. If that were true, then I'd be talking to a ghost. The flight attendant who handed you that pillow would have been talking to a ghost."

Even as she said it, Jenna had to admit that George certainly looked dead. He was deathly pale and had perspired so much in the last twenty-four hours he had no more water weight, only bones. And his skin had tightened, what might have been the perfect facelift if it hadn't revealed so much of his skull.

He said, "None of the dreams—at least the ones I can remember—none of them are about things before the train wreck."

"What kind of dreams?" Jenna asked.

"Nightmares, really. What happened at that New Age shop... and that man trying to choke you after the accident."

"Any dreams of your wife?"

"No. Which is what I find so troubling. When Carri died, I felt like I had lost everything, except my life, and my memories of her. Now I can't even dream of her...."

Jenna had forgotten she had rested her hand on George's, which felt no more substantial than thin air, as if he really were a ghost. But now after his painful admission, she squeezed it and felt the meat of it, if not the warmth.

"She's there," Jenna said. "That's just how dreams are. Sometimes you don't remember who's in them."

George nodded, but didn't say anything. Jenna tried to read his reaction, but couldn't. Body language depended heavily on the eyes, and his were so different now, she found it near impossible to find any social cue there.

"The code on that last page," he said, indicating her notebook. "What's it called again?"

"*Lingua Ignota*," she said. "The unknown language. An abbess, Hildegard of Bingen... she created it. You're probably familiar with some of her hymns, actually."

"Why's it unknown?" George said.

"Depends on who you ask. Some think Hildegard created it to make her Rupertsberg nuns stand apart from other converts; kind of a divine aristocracy. But there's also the school of thought that it's simply a reminder of the spiritual unknown; legend has it that God passed the language down to Hildegard from on high. Personally, I like to think it's really a map to the lost paradise."

"Eden?"

"Right."

"So if it's a secret language, how'd this guy get it? The author of the Codex."

"Well, Herman... he was a monk of the same order as Hildegard. And he lived pretty close to where she created it. So it's likely he had access to it."

"You said the language came from God."

"Actually, I said that's the legend."

"Well, just to throw this out there," George said, "what if Herman also got the code from God?"

Jenna thought about it. A few days ago, she would have rejected the notion, but she at least was willing to consider the perspective. "I guess it doesn't matter. It's here now. We have to deal with it."

"Good point. So did you finish decoding it?"

Around the cabin, a few of the business-class passengers began to stir. The plane was approaching London, and flight attendants were coming around to collect trash.

"Yes," Jenna said. "It's definitely an exorcism."

She let George study what she had translated.

"How's your memory?" he asked.

"Good. Actually, pretty damn good. Why?"

"Because you need to start memorizing this. The quatrains, this exorcism—all of it."

"Word for word?"

"Yes. And I'll do the same."

As a flight attendant approached them, George began to wrap the bloody pillow in the blanket. "Problem is, I may not be here much longer. So you have to memorize everything. Perfectly."

He stuffed the wrapped pillow underneath the seat in front of him just as the flight attendant came to check for any trash. Jenna dismissed her politely.

When they were alone again, Jenna said, "If that's the case, I think we need a second opinion on the translation. Some of this stuff's pretty ambiguous, so I think... I think we need to see Raymond."

"Are you sure?"

"No, I'm not sure. And I've had the entire flight to London to convince myself that it's absolutely the wrong decision. But as long as we're careful about the circumstances in meeting with him, and because I think he could really help with interpreting these quatrains, I've sort of mentally justified the risk of bringing him into the picture."

"Then you need to get ahold of him as soon as you can use your phone."

Jenna nodded, and thought about what she would say to Raymond. Telling him she was in possession of the missing Codex Gigas pages would surely get him in a cab, even if he was in the middle of having sex with a woman. Telling him she was interested in going on a date with him would probably get him out of bed... but only after he had finished sex with the woman. Telling him nothing except that he might die if he helped her would be the right thing to say, but it was also the one tactic she wasn't sure how he would respond. If he was in the middle of having sex with a woman, then all bets were off. She would have no idea what he would do.

"Jenna, you need to start memorizing the pages now," George said. He had expected her to begin immediately after he had raised the subject, but was disturbed to watch her stare off into space.

"Yes, George, I'm on it."

"Okay, if you say so. But, Jenna, just so we're clear, you need to memorize all the pages... as if your life depended on it."

"Because it does," Jenna said. "Yeah, George, I got it."

CHAPTER 29

A TEXT MESSAGE WOKE RAYMOND UP. It was Jenna. He knew because of the custom ringtone, which he had sampled from their radio show and had edited it to say, "This is Jenna Grant... *Stripped and Exposed.*"

I want to see you, she had written.

Why? he wrote back. *What's wrong?*

I'm in trouble. But chance u will be in the shit if u help. Trust me, better off just ignoring. But if u still want to help, here's what to do...

As per Jenna's instructions, Raymond went to the Riser Café on Oxford Street and sat at a table with a clear view of the entrance. He was waiting for a man named George.

With a seat so close to the kitchen, he didn't trust that he would hear his phone over all the clattering of dishes and the shouting of the chef and cooks; so he set the phone to vibrate and held onto it. He ordered kippers and crumpet, but lost his appetite; the smell, though delicious, made him queasy this early in the morning.

"Raymond?" someone asked. "Raymond Chappell?"

Historically, Oxford Street served as a sort of green mile for condemned men traveling from Newgate Prison to the old Tyburn gallows. This man approaching his table, sweaty and pale as a corpse, looked like he, too, was walking his last mile.

The man held Jenna's smartphone, and when he hit a button on the keypad, Raymond's cell lit up with a picture of her, sipping one of her silly drinks she had brought with her from the States. He had taken the picture at Gerry's Pub after their very first show together.

"My name is George," the pale man said.

Raymond stood, not even caring when he knocked his knee on the table. "Is Jenna okay?"

"Yes. But we need to go."

Raymond threw a tip on the table and then grabbed his bag. He followed George through the kitchen of the café.

"What the bloody hell?" the chef said, but George and Raymond were already hurrying out the back exit into the alleyway.

A black cab sat waiting for them. George held the door open for Raymond, but stopped him before he got in.

"Are you sure you want to do this?"

"Yes, mate, of course. If Jenna's in trouble, then I want to help."

"She told you how dangerous it is?"

"Yes. Now come on, the meter's running." And with that, Raymond hopped into the cab.

———

AFTER TAKING THE HEATHROW EXPRESS from the airport to Paddington Station, Jenna and George had parted ways. Jenna had taken a series of black cabs to throw off anyone who might have been following
her, but eventually she ended up back at the station. It connected directly to the Hilton Paddington London Hotel, where Jenna used her credit
card to rent the Hilton's only vacancy, an expensive King Junior Suite.
She took the elevator up to her room.

Even though she had washed up with a paper towel after their run-in
with the blonde, Jenna felt grimy, stained. And she could still smell
blood, as if some had gotten into her nostril. So now, for the first time
since leaving Cambridge, she took the chance to shower.

The hot water soothed her bruises; it felt great on her back and in
her hair. She loved the flowery shampoo, the citrusy soap. She loved
the slick suds on her belly and breast. She even got a chance to run a
razor over her legs. By the time she got out, bare feet smacking on the
marble, she felt like a new person.

Jenna changed into some clothes and was in the middle of running a
brush through her hair when she heard a knock on the door.

Probably just George, she thought. George, but no Raymond. She
could almost convince herself that her co-host had bailed on her, if she
hadn't been calculating the odds. She thought it was 60-40 in favor of
Raymond showing up at the café. And she based her calculations solely
on the belief that Raymond was too terrified and suspicious that her
early morning text-plea was a prank by one of his pub buddies, and that
if he didn't appear as instructed, he would look like a "wanker"—not
her choice of nouns, but the term she thought would be running through

Raymond's head. She had tried to communicate to him the seriousness of the request by ending the original text message with the words, *NO JOKE. SERIOUS HERE.*

At the door of her hotel room, she leaned over and peeked out of the peephole. Immediately her heart started pounding at the sight.

Quickly, she unlocked the door. And because it had been a while that her face had matched what she was actually feeling, Jenna did her best to grin as she threw open the door.

"So you weren't kidding," Raymond said. "This is some sort of spy novel you're involved in."

"I wish I was kidding," Jenna replied.

He wanted to hug her, but didn't make a move; they had never really physically embraced before. So Jenna, not as reserved, threw her arms around him. In fact, she hugged him so tightly he feared she would reinjure the vertebrae in his lower back, which he had initially damaged in prep school when he was foolish enough to try rugby.

When Jenna finally let go, Raymond noticed the tears in her eyes. For the first time he began to take seriously what he had committed to so cavalierly earlier in the morning. But George nipped any of his misgivings in the bud when he put his hand on Raymond's shoulder and nudged him into the room.

———

WITHOUT SAYING ANYTHING ABOUT WHY they had gathered at the hotel, Jenna gave the men a tour of the room, trying her best to ease Raymond into the situation by making singsong comments about the Art

Deco décor, and by responding to his compliments about her gift-shop clothes.

All George could hear was Jenna delaying the inevitable. He was surprised by the "padded landing" approach she had decided to employ with Raymond. From everything he had witnessed on the ride over to the hotel, her co-host was sturdy enough to handle whatever she needed to tell him about the events in the last forty-eight hours. George managed to keep his objections to himself until her tour threatened to stretch out to the room's terrace and the view.

"Why don't we hold that for later," he said, reining her in from the sliding glass door. "Don't you think it's best we get Raymond up to speed?"

Jenna nodded and led Raymond over to two easy chairs flanking a tall, round cocktail table. George sat on the bed.

"I don't know if you saw it on the news over here," Jenna began, "but... my brother, Neal, he did something terrible. It's hard to speak about it aloud, so I guess it's best I just say it straight out. He drove a car that I was a passenger in... He actually steered it directly into the path of a commuter train."

"The one in Virginia?" Raymond said. "That was your brother?"

Jenna nodded. "I haven't gotten the latest casualty report, and there's probably a gutless reason why I haven't done so. Maybe it has something to do with the fact that my brother is responsible for the deaths of so many innocent people; it's almost impossible for me to face what he's done."

She stopped talking, stiff except for her trembling lips and hands.

George noticed Raymond couldn't maintain eye contact with Jenna as she told her story. During critical points in her speech, his attention flashed to the balcony. Then he turned to the carpet. And by the time Jenna had finished relating her painful experience, Raymond's eyes had somehow wound up on George.

Finally, after an uncomfortably long silence, Raymond looked at Jenna.

"I think I understand. But I just want to make sure I get the details right. Jenna, your own brother tried to kill you?"

"I almost wish he had killed me."

"Please don't say that. At least not around me."

"I just meant, at least I wouldn't have to face the horrible, inevitable stories sure to follow about the lives my brother has destroyed."

Raymond's eyes once again drifted toward the window. This time his silence was not so long. "I hope you don't mind, but I think I need a drink."

When no one objected, Raymond got up and helped himself to a beer from the mini fridge. After a few generous gulps, he made his way back to the chair.

From the look on Raymond's face, George figured he probably thought Jenna was done relating her dreadful experience. But then she started back up again, detailing the events after the train collision, including the attack in Occoquan. It was as if Jenna had come back onstage for an encore even though her audience had barely survived the main performance.

Raymond listened silently again. George thought maybe he was waiting to react until Jenna was truly finished.

"Raymond, are you all right?" she asked.

"No, I'm probably not all right. But that's mostly because I'm worried about you."

George was impressed with Raymond's response. But he also noted that Jenna's co-host was in the middle of his second beer by the time he expressed his concern for her well-being.

As emotionally vacuous as her retelling of their nightmare had been, Jenna now put all of her emotions into reassuring him that their current situation was somehow different. "Don't worry. Everything I just described is in the past tense. I'm totally fine now, Raymond, I promise you."

Raymond gulped down the last of his second beer, and Jenna looked over at George. She suspected they both had the same thoughts: the second beer was for the road.

Her co-host was leaving, catching the next train back to Cambridge. And he would try his best to pretend that her phone text for help, and everything afterward, was all part of a feverish hangover dream.

But then Raymond cleared his throat and dispelled their doubts. "Well then, I'm dying to see the pages. I feel at this point I've come close enough to earning the privilege."

Jenna couldn't help but smile. She knew there was a reason she and Raymond got along so well.

No surface in the room except for the bed was big enough to spread out the pages from the Codex Gigas. George relocated to one of the easy chairs, and Raymond stared wide-eyed as Jenna laid out the artifact on the coverlet. Before she was even done, he was reaching into the plastic sleeve of the first page to touch the cured animal hide.

"Raymond, you should put on some gloves."

"Sorry," he said as he touched the parchment anyway. After he withdrew his finger, he said, "I should feel ashamed, but I don't. You can't touch the pages under glass in Sweden."

She asked him to perform a few tests to further authenticate the pages, and he, too, concluded that they were genuine. Then he pulled one of the easy chairs up to the bed and began to compare the translations in Jenna's notebook to the Latin on the ancient skin. Here and there, he wrote a few notes.

While he worked, Jenna paced back and forth in front of the glass doors to the terrace. George watched the flat-screen TV on mute; more coverage of the earthquake in Syria.

"These quatrains," Raymond said. "They're undeniably referencing the Bible. Don't you agree?"

"Yes," Jenna replied, "I believe so. The Vulgate version of the Bible was part of the original Codex Gigas, so it makes sense for Herman to reference it. What stanzas are you seeing it in?"

"What stanza am I *not* seeing it in? Take quatrain four for example. He uses the words *famine and locusts*, which are both likely to be references to the Apocalypse from the Book of Revelation. Then in the fifth quatrain, there's the phrase *Angelic light*. Which is interesting because, in Corinthians, Angel of Light is just another name for Lucifer."

Jenna glanced over at George, who nodded and then turned back to the news.

"Did I say something stupid?" Raymond asked.

"Absolutely not," Jenna said. "Keep going."

He flipped back through the notebook. "Okay, good, because I find the first quatrain even more supportive of my theory. The first part reads: 'It was upon the fall when the light / From the morning star came upon me.' Obviously, Herman could be using the word *fall* as a reference to the season of the year, but setting aside that euphemisms such as *fall* for *autumn* may not have existed in thirteenth-century Eastern

Europe, the use of the word *fall*, closely followed by the phrase *morning star*, I believe leads to one very safe conclusion. Herman must be referencing Satan's fall from grace. Isaiah 14:12, 'How you have fallen from heaven, O morning star, son of the dawn! You have been cast down to the earth, you once laid low the nations! You said in your heart, 'I will ascend to heaven; I will raise my throne above the stars of God.''

Jenna had stopped pacing as she listened to the passage. "Mighty impressive."

"Thanks," Raymond said. "Though I must admit you would be the first woman I've ever been attracted to that quoting a major section of the Bible has elicited a positive response. On all other occasions, it's pretty much cleared the room."

Jenna suppressed a smile. "Okay, so what else?"

Raymond turned to another page of translations. "How about the seventh quatrain? Where else besides the world of sadomasochism is *the Restrainer* a prominent phrase, except for in the Holy Bible? I'm afraid I can't cite exact chapter and verse, but—"

Jenna, who had resumed pacing, said, "'For the secret power of lawlessness is already at work; but the one who now holds it back will continue to do so till he is taken out of the way. And then the lawless one will be revealed.'"

Raymond smiled. "Touché."

"It's Thessalonians," Jenna said. "Chapter two. Can't remember which verse."

"Still, you've obviously done your homework," he said.

"A bit. I wanted to know what I was getting into. And I wanted to know if we came to the same conclusion independently."

"Very scientific of you. So as long as we're being objective, I must admit a prejudice, the same one I have against my father's profession: what relevance do passages from the Bible, or anything that a monk wrote in the thirteenth century, have to anyone living in our century?"

Jenna stopped pacing. "I've been struggling with that same question myself."

"Well, you're probably like me and assumed the biblical stuff you'd discover would be embedded in rock," Raymond said, "not in some CNN headline. Don't you agree?"

"Oh, of course. Herman's quatrains would have been very relevant to me, but not beyond the dig. Interesting, but not relevant—not to my life."

"The dig *is* your life," Raymond pointed out, and she took a second to think about that. He was right: her two lives had always been interconnected. And now that they had collided, it was even harder to tell her life apart from the wreck.

George turned his attention from the TV. "If the question concerning the pages is their relevance, then perhaps it'd be more productive tying some of these quatrains to current events."

Raymond leaned back in his chair and laced his hands behind his head. "I'm game. But it's exactly like people who interpret Nostradamus's quatrains: the material's so ambiguous and vague, it can quickly turn into seeing what you want to see."

"Or what you want to believe," Jenna added, pacing again. "But let's do it anyway."

Raymond looked over the translations. "Okay then. Shall we begin with the French ambassador? You obviously think he plugs into all this."

"Actually, I think Tottone was just a pawn. I don't even think he ranks a mention in the quatrains."

Raymond nodded, but Jenna could tell she had thrown him off his game. He scanned the translations for a while, eyebrows knitted in concentration.

"Okay, maybe I've had too much to drink, but someone else needs to get us started. Suggest a current event." He didn't sound frustrated, but more like he was playing a game of Spot the Fake. Jenna was glad for that. Frustration would only lead to weariness, and they couldn't afford to be weary.

"How about the attempted assassination of John Wolfenson?" George suggested, pointing at the muted TV, where a dozen microphones were shoved into the envoy's face.

"Quartet to the Middle East, right?" Raymond said.

"Yes," Jenna replied, crossing her arms. She wished she had told George not to mention it. Raymond needed to come up with the same theory independently. Nevertheless, she understood why George might be operating on a faster timeline than her scientific methods allowed.

Raymond said, "I saw Wolfenson on one of the news talk shows recently. He's become quite the celebrity. And not just in Great Britain. He's everywhere."

Jenna stopped pacing and stood at the glass doors leading to the balcony. "Okay, so you know who he is. Do you see any quatrains that might apply?"

Raymond looked at the pages. "Yeah, the seventh."

Jenna nodded. "'But a fatal wound invites his light / An astonished world is a witness / As an emissary of peace is resurrected.'"

"Hmm, close," Raymond said. "It's not *emissary* here, it's *messenger*."

"Damn it," she said, coming over to look. "You're right. *Emissary* is later."

Raymond caught Jenna and George sharing a worried look; he didn't quite understand the issue, but all of this was a little over his head anyway.

"I don't know about over in the States," he said, "but after the attack on Wolfenson, all the London papers were calling him a messenger of peace. I specifically remember one of the tabloids using the word *resurrected*. Thought it was a bit heavy-handed, myself. A little bit preachy."

"So," Jenna said, back to her pacing, "are we saying Herman was writing poetry to predict what would happen hundreds of years later?"

Raymond sat back in his chair. "Yeah, I guess if we want to discuss whether people like Herman or Nostradamus are truly accurate weathermen. And in that case, I need another pint."

Jenna marched over to the fridge and looked inside. "Sorry, we're all out of Bass Pale Ale."

"Then the Newcastle Brown will have to do."

She gave him the bottle, and he opened it, enjoying the crisp pop and hiss of carbonation, and the taste.

On TV, the news had switched to the devastation in Aleppo. Jenna pointed it out to Raymond.

"That's convenient," he said, holding up a finger as he checked the ninth translation. "We were just talking about how an ancient city would fall. What are the bloody odds of that?"

Jenna gave him a sober look. "This news has been on all day, Raymond. I wouldn't read too much into it."

George, who had barely spoken, said, "Aleppo is where John Wolfenson is headed. To help with the earthquake effort."

"Hang on, that sort of makes sense," Raymond said. "In quatrain eight, where it says, 'The Emissary prepares his flock / They will fly toward the sun / The blind and—'"

"'... deceived trapped in their beaks,'" Jenna added.

"Right. Well, *Emissary* is how you've translated the Latin, *legatus*. But it could've easily been *Envoy*."

"True. But if Wolfenson's really the Emissary, then what we're talking about is serious. Read the eleventh stanza. He's planning some pretty nasty stuff."

Raymond flipped through the notebook to that page, but Jenna had already begun to quote it.

"'From the seed he has planted / A slithering root will grow / The Serpent will be watered from oceans of blood / And fertilized by the bones of the beasts.'"

"Excellent," Raymond said. "Perfect recitation. You didn't even peek."

George had noticed, too, and felt relieved after the scare Jenna's first mistake had given him. Perhaps she hadn't exaggerated her ability to memorize after all.

"So..." Raymond said, "are we suggesting that after his attack, John Wolfenson is somehow working for the devil?"

Jenna leaned back against the glass doors, eyes closed. She let out a deep sigh and said, "Believe me, I know how it sounds. But I'm almost positive that's what my brother must have thought. He and whoever he was working for."

Finally, Raymond turned to George. "What do you think, mate?"

George held out his hand and said, "I think I want one of those beers you've been drinking."

———

THEY CONTINUED FOR HOURS, comparing each quatrain to recent events. They didn't want to take a chance calling room service, so they raided the refrigerator for all of its sandwiches, potato chips, and finger foods. They also drank the rest of the beer and a bottle of white wine.

"What about the tenth quatrain?" Raymond asked. "I find that to be a real puzzle." He read the stanza aloud, trying not to slur his words. "'His veiled plan calls for raising nineteen / And they will cast their sleepy eyes / On the most beautiful of jewels / Rebuilding a house on shattered sacred stone.'" He looked up at Jenna. "Any recent events tie into that?"

"No, not really. But I think I've figured out the straight-up interpretation of what it means."

"Oh yeah? Give me a hint."

"'The most beautiful of jewels' and 'sacred stone' seem to suggest we're at a gem convention. But what if we thought differently?"

Raymond engaged his brain, but after a couple of minutes he turned to Jenna, looking embarrassed. "I need another hint."

"Fair enough. Let's look at the phrase 'raising nineteen.' Other than raising a family, what other context is the word *raising* used?"

"Raising Cain!" Raymond shouted, smiling. "No, wait... Raising the dead."

"Right. And the next line has the words 'sleepy eyes.' The word *sleep* is often used in the Bible to signify death. So if we trust that the references in this quatrain, along with the other quatrains, play off the Bible, then 'the most beautiful of jewels' is a reference to what?"

Raymond thought for a few moments, but then shook his head. "I guess it's a reference to how much I've drunk because nothing's coming to me."

"Don't beat yourself up. If I'm right, the Biblical reference is not a wildly popular one. 'The most beautiful of jewels' is from Ezekiel 16:7. It's a euphemism for the city of Jerusalem."

"You really have done your homework," Raymond said. "So, we have the walking dead casting their sleepy eyes on Jerusalem. But who are the nineteen? And what in the bloody hell is the shattered sacred stone?"

"I have no idea who the nineteen are, but I have some thoughts about the sacred stone."

Jenna looked over at George. His eyes were closed. And he didn't appear to be breathing.

"Oh no... George?" She walked over and shook his shoulder. "George!"

He sprang upright in the easy chair, shouting, "What?! What's wrong?"

"Oh, thank God," Jenna said, laying a hand over her pounding heart. "I thought you were gone."

"No. Just resting my eyes," he said. "Any more progress?"

"Not with tying in current events," Raymond said, moving his chair so that he sat opposite George. "The only quatrains that seem to correlate with Wolfenson and the Aleppo earthquake are the seventh and the ninth. Nothing else seems to match anything in the news."

"Then perhaps all the quatrains before the seventh one pre-date the attack on Wolfenson," George said.

Jenna nodded. "You might be right."

George stretched his arms and yawned. Besides thinking more clearly, he looked ten times better. The short rest had done him well.

"Why don't you both take a break," he said. "Take that tour of the balcony or something. We've still got a few more hours before calling it a night."

"Are you sure you're okay?" Jenna asked.

"Yeah, I'm just going to sit here and rest some more until you come back in."

Jenna nodded, and then she and Raymond went out onto the terrace. The cool breeze reminded her of how warm and weary she felt, and the view from the sixth floor reminded her of how small. Over the gables of St. Mary's hospital, they could see the steel and glass building of Marks & Spencer, the tower cranes near the wharf. Over Norfolk Towers, they could see the lights of the West End.

Because of her mother and her career as an archeologist, Jenna had travelled all over the world. She had witnessed Cairo sunrises, Kauai sunsets. She was no longer easily impressed. But sometimes it wasn't just the view, but who she was with, and the circumstances. Out here on the terrace, she could finally relax.

Raymond had his hands on the balcony railing and was staring out at the city, his dirty-blond hair stirring in the breeze. Jenna leaned her back against the railing next to him.

"I probably haven't told you how much your help means to me," she said.

"Sure you have. I do have to say, though, if you'd told me we'd be staying in such a lovely room, I wouldn't have hesitated at all."

"What're you talking about? You didn't hesitate when I contacted you."

"Oh, didn't I?" He turned to her with a smile. "I thought surely I had."

"Actually you should have said, 'No, I won't help you. Now please lose my number.'"

"Is that what you would have done?"

"Maybe."

"I'm not buying it. You would have been too intrigued by the pages. There's no way you would have turned down that opportunity."

Jenna thought about it for a moment. "Is that why you're here? For the pages?"

"Screw the Codex Gigas," he said, turning to face her. "I don't care if Herman *did* write it in a single night. I bet he was juiced on steroids the whole time anyway."

"So then why are you here?"

"Just what I told you. I'm worried about you."

Jenna stared into his eyes with the hint of a smile on her lips. From past experience, she knew when she maintained eye contact like this, the guy would either get a clue and kiss her, or he would look away.

Raymond looked away. "Maybe we should go back inside and check on your friend," he said. His right fist was clenched, as if he were angry.

Can't blame him, Jenna thought. Combing through the quatrains for the past few hours, he had probably realized just how deeply Jenna had involved him in something extremely dangerous. He had said he was worried about her, but it was a verbal sleight of hand—he was actually worried about himself. And here she was trying to kiss him?

"You know what continues to bother me?" he said, turning back to face her.

Here it comes, she thought.

"Quatrain two, the third line."

Surprised, Jenna couldn't immediately remember the quote. "'Or long enough to rite this injustice'—is that correct?"

"That's the one. Your translation of the word *rite* was accurate. Herman intentionally used the Latin *ritus*, which means *rite* or *ritual*. But in the context of the sentence, it would seem appropriate to use the Latin word *rectus*, which means *correct*, or *right*."

"I noticed the same thing," she said, wishing they were doing something other than talking about the pages. Romantically, poetry had never done much for Jenna. "The word initially got me to question my knowledge of Latin. But what's your point?"

"The use of the word *rite* on pages adjacent to an exorcism? That can't be coincidence."

Jenna nodded. "Couldn't agree more."

"So, if Herman's quatrains are true and they point to some end-of-the-world scenario, that means you've got yourself in the middle of some Satan vs. God smackdown."

"You mean I got us both in the middle of it."

"I'm not worried about myself. What I want to know is if you really believe all this is true?"

Jenna turned around and looked out at the West End. She felt like they had gone over this a hundred times, and she still wasn't certain. "If it's not true, then how come so many people are running around like it's the end of the world?"

Raymond shrugged. "I wish I had a rational explanation." He stepped up and placed his hand next to hers on the railing. "That's why I'm worried about you."

"Well," Jenna said, "if it is the end of the world, we should've picked a better view."

"Hmm, I fear that bottle of wine is making you glib. The last thing you should be feeling right now is glib."

Jenna turned to face him. He stood so close that she could smell the beer and wine on his breath, and his familiar but fading cologne. She stared into his eyes again, and this time he didn't look away, but nor did he make a move.

"Oh God," Jenna said, "will you shut up and kiss me before I change my mind?"

Raymond grinned. He leaned down and kissed her, and Jenna could feel the shape of the smile still on his lips, could feel every inch of space between them and the street below, all six stories of space. For the first time in a long time, her brain shut off and she let her body take control.

———

PRETENDING TO SLEEP, George kept one eye parted so slightly that his eyelashes blurred his vision. He watched Jenna and Raymond until he was satisfied they wouldn't be coming back in for a few minutes. Then he climbed out of the easy chair, struggling like an old man.

From the bed, he gathered up the Codex Gigas pages, along with Jenna's translations. As he carried everything toward the bathroom, he looked out onto the terrace. What he saw there was beautiful, something in which Carri might have found some artful angle: two people embracing against the backdrop of a city much older and larger than either of them, yet not nearly as timeless and breathtaking as a kiss.

George let them be and stepped into the bathroom. He locked the door behind him.

Earlier that day, when he and Jenna had separated at the train station, George had bought lighter fluid and a pack of matches. He dumped the notebook and the pages into the bathtub and lightly doused everything in the flammable fluid. Then he struck a match and tossed it in.

Clutching the handicap rail, he sat on the toilet and watched centuries of history burn and become lost again to time.

———

ACROSS FROM THE HILTON, on the corner of Praed and London, Etan Vlessel leaned against a black railing where bicyclists typically chained their bikes. Commuters raced back and forth on the sidewalk behind him, either to the bus stop, or to the hotel to catch a train. They paid very little notice to Etan as he peered through a small pair of night-vision binoculars.

On a terrace high on the sixth floor of the Hilton, the woman from the wreck was sharing a passionate kiss with some blond man. Etan rarely saw two people so happy to be oblivious and vulnerable. The fools truly thought they were safe under the cloak of night.

He smiled as he lowered the binoculars and grabbed his phone from his coat. He typed out a message and sent it to his employer. The message read, *I have eyes on our target. There's another player involved...*

THE STORY CONTINUES in *DEMON DAYS - BOOK THREE*

ACKNOWLEDGEMENTS

D.L. SNELL

Thanks to Dr. Kim Paffenroth for the Latin, and both Zeinah Abunuwar and Ahmad Al-Shakarji for the Arabic. And thanks to Krakenten for the invaluable lesson in firearms. Also, I would like to acknowledge all the fans of the first book: without you... well, without you we'd still go on writing, but it would be a lonely, lonely business.

RICHARD FINNEY

I want to express my appreciation for the feedback and invaluable support of Jay Frasco. Emily Finney was so very helpful with her research. Of course none of this would have been possible without the support of David and the rest of the fine people at Ape Entertainment. And a special thanks to Danuta Skulski, who read the first half of this book overnight. Her enthusiasm for the story and her desire to read the rest of the book kept me writing.

ABOUT THE AUTHORS

RICHARD FINNEY is a Los Angeles based writer and film producer.

Visit his website -- richardfinney.blogspot.com

D.L. SNELL is a novelist, a member of the Horror Writers Association, and a freelance editor for Permuted Press. He has sold short stories to anthologies such as Pocket Books' *Blood Lite* series, and his first novel *Roses of Blood on Barbwire Vines* pits zombies against vampires. Author Nicholas Grabowsky has called Snell's work "damn good writing."

WRITTEN BY RICHARD FINNEY

DEMON DAYS
DEMON DAYS – BOOK TWO
DEMON DAYS – BOOK THREE
DEMON DAYS – BOOK FOUR

RELICT
BOOK ONE – DRAWING BLOOD
BOOK TWO – SHADOWS IN THE LIGHT (2013)

BLACK MARIAH
BOOK ONE - A CALLING (2013)